THE HOTWIFE'S FREEUSE FANTASY

5 Stories of Office Temptation

The Freeuse Plaything
Freeuse Office Slut
Freeuse Office Games
Freeuse Office Hours
Freeuse Office Party

Lacey Cross

Paperback ISBN: 978-1-960162-36-6

CONTENTS

The Freeuse Plaything

Watching Her Take It

Lacey Cross

Chapter 1

It's 8:05, and I'm sitting in my car in the parking lot of the lawyer's office I've worked at for years. I'm already late, so another few minutes won't matter. I should have just called in sick. My mood is particularly low today.

It's a dreary morning, and the rain is an annoying mist that I know is going to coat me as soon as I step out of my car. I picked up a latte from the local coffee stand this morning, and I blame the coffee for my mood. My usual cafe shut down last week, and the new place is serving swill.

Sighing, I give up. As I get out of the car, I swear the mist makes me damp instantly. Yep, called it.

I need to just go in to work and forget about my boring life. I'm thirty-four years old, and if I'm not careful, I might blink and be forty-five, still working at the same firm. Fuck, what am I doing?

Jon and I decided a year ago that we didn't want kids yet, and we went through the process to freeze some of my eggs. We're not sure if we're ever going to want kids, but now we have some options down the road if we need them. I always assumed I'd take a few years off if we had a kid, but is this going to be my life now if we don't? Working here forever?

Grabbing my purse and lunch sack, I scurry across the parking lot and into the building. The receptionist, Cindy, has an uncharacteristically huge smile on her face, and I don't want to deal with her happiness this morning.

I force a tight smile and greet her with a cheery, "Good morning," as I continue down the hallway. I wish I could say I felt as chipper as my tone, but I'm an emotional mess this morning, and I don't like how grumpy I am. Is it time to move on?

I've been considering finding a new job, and maybe my mood means it's time to pull the trigger. There's just one problem. I make a lot of money here, and it would be near impossible to find a job that pays as well. Come to find out, if you fuck all your bosses, they make sure you're happy with your salary. That was never my intention when I started fucking them six years ago, but it's been a nice perk.

The sexy stuff ended a couple of years ago, which might be part of my job dissatisfaction. A new lawyer, Mr. King, joined the firm, and I had an amazing week of being his freeuse office toy.

Then, a week later, they opened up a position for an office manager, and they hired a woman named Bonny who ended up being a stickler for rules. I don't know what Bonny heard, but her first meeting with me included information about not fraternizing with people in the office. The new policies put an end to all the fun times at work. Somehow, I doubt Cindy got the same talk.

I just need a change of scenery—maybe a trip. It's the beginning of December, so it's not the optimal time to book a vacation, but perhaps after the new year, Jon will take a weekend getaway with me. Some vacation sex should boost my spirits.

Just as I settle into my chair and slide my purse into my desk drawer, Cindy saunters over to me, wearing a mischievous grin. "Have you heard the news?" she asks.

I like Cindy—I really do—but I'm not in the mood for games this morning, so I turn on my computer and give her my serious tone. "No, tell me."

Cindy's eyes light up with excitement. "When I arrived at work today, everyone was in a meeting in the conference room with Bonny."

She's got my attention now, and I tip my head, interested. "Really? Do you know what it was about?"

"Yes and no," she replies, still smiling. "But when the meeting was over, Bonny packed up her desk and left."

My mind races with possibilities. "Is she gone for good?"

Cindy nods triumphantly. "Yep, she was fired."

Cindy and I may not see eye to eye all the time, but our shared disdain for Bonny's changes has bound us together in animosity. Cindy didn't like how she couldn't leave early whenever she wanted anymore, and I was annoyed by not being able to fuck the lawyers. Not quite the same thing, but this new development won't break either of our hearts.

My desk phone rings, and as I answer, Cindy gives me a little wave and departs. I spend the next few minutes dealing with questions from another law firm about a bounced email. When I finish, I'm still in a daze, contemplating the implications of Bonny's sudden departure.

I take a sip of my coffee, now oblivious to its unpleasant taste. I could fuck my bosses again if we all wanted to, but do I? And more importantly, would Jon let me?

It's been over a year since I've slept with someone else. Jon and I never said we were finished with me being a hotwife, but once easy access to my bosses' cocks was gone, I was content to snuggle up with Jon at home instead of hunting for other men to fuck. It's not that Jon isn't satisfying me, but lately our love life has been growing stale again. He's not in the mood as often anymore, and I blame stress from his job. He's only five years older than me, but I know stress can dampen a man's libido.

Jon might be okay with less sex, but lately I've been running to grab a sex toy whenever I'm alone in the house. A girl's got needs, and mine seem to be increasing right when his are decreasing. Whose bright idea was it to mismatch women's and men's sex drives? Fucking human biology.

I spend my morning fantasizing about the good old days when I'd sashay into work late and receive a spanking as punishment. What if I could have that again?

My pussy is already soaked when lunchtime rolls around. I settle in at a table in the breakroom, clutching a bottle of water and a container of leftover pasta. But before I dig in, I send Jon a text.

Miranda:

> So...can I fuck my bosses again?

I follow it up with a puppy GIF with pleading eyes to sweeten the deal. I'm not expecting him to turn me down, but if he even hesitates, I won't do it. We're in this together, or I'm out. He texts back immediately.

Jon:

> What about Bonny?

That wasn't the response I hoped for. I wanted him to be thrilled and then ask about the specifics.

Miranda:

> She was fired today, and I don't know why. This is all my idea. No one asked that I fuck them. I wanted to talk to you first.

Shit, I should have waited until I got home to have this conversation with him. I take a sip of water, intending to suggest we discuss it later, when a message with an image attached pops up. It's a picture of my husband's slacks, focused at his crotch. Rusty—the nickname my husband gave his cock—is evidently hard beneath his pants.

Jon:

> Rusty approves of you fucking your bosses, and you know he makes the decisions around here.

My sudden laughter makes me spit water over my pasta. *Damn, Miranda, smooth move there.* I grab a paper towel and reply.

Miranda:

> Well, my pussy says she wants to be filled up by someone besides her owner. Are you in agreement with Rusty?

His reply makes my body hum and my heart rate speed up.

Jon:

> Go to town. Have fun, Kitten, and fill up on some fresh cream. You can tell me all about it while I fuck you later. Text me when you have some news.

Look at that, just talking about fucking my bosses again has Jon ready to go to pound town. Bonny should have left months ago.

Miranda:

> Thank you, my love!

It's time to find Mr. Jacobs and offer myself to him. He's the big boss; it's only right he gets first dibs.

CHAPTER 2

I want to surprise Mr. Jacobs, so I don't ask to speak with him first before showing up at his office door. Straightening the hem of my pencil skirt, I adjust the front of my pink blouse and try to calm the butterflies in my stomach. I'm glad I chose this outfit today, since I'm also wearing sexy lace underwear and a garter belt with black stockings to make myself feel good. If Mr. Jacobs gets to see them, I'll consider my mood brightened.

He calls out, "Come in."

I straighten my shoulders and sway my hips as I enter. I'm flushed and hope my face isn't as pink as my blouse. It's been way too long since he's bent me over his desk, and just seeing him behind it makes my nipples harden.

I'm not the same naïve woman who once sat before him and negotiated how fucking all the lawyers here would work. Now I'm a woman who knows how to get what she wants. And this slut wants Daddy Jacobs's cock inside her as soon as possible.

Mr. Jacobs is in his late 50s, and his hair is more salt than pepper these days. He wears it well. I've definitely got a kink for men in charge. His usual poker face shows his surprise when, instead of sitting in a chair, I walk behind his desk and perch on the edge next to him. My flirtatious smile blossoms slowly as I cross my legs, letting my skirt ride up. The edge of my stockings shows, and I notice his gaze flick down towards my legs before returning to look me in the eye.

Oh yeah, I know what Mr. Jacobs likes. We're playing my game now.

His voice is stern. "I was about to call you in here. We need to talk."

I lean forward, knowing it puts my cleavage on display, and walk my fingers up the front of his white button-down shirt. I fiddle with the top button, pretending that I'm going to open it. He's not wearing a full suit, but he still gets my pussy buzzing. He doesn't need to wear a jacket and tie to make me want to fuck him.

"Do we?" I pout. "I can think of better things to do with our time now that Bonny's gone."

Mr. Jacobs's face darkens. Oops, did I push him too far and he's going to scold me? Mmm, wait, I like what he does when I misbehave. This is going to all work out just fine.

Mr. Jacobs doesn't disappoint. In a deep, commanding voice, he orders me, "Up and over, slut."

Liquid pools in my center, and I quiver with excitement as I roll off the edge and turn around so I can bend over his desk. I lift my hips and press my ass toward him as he stands. He expertly unzips my skirt, and I sigh in delight as it drops to my feet. I'm getting whiplash from how quickly my sucky day has turned into the best workday in months.

He plays with the edge of my stockings and glides his fingers up my garter belt until he reaches my ass. His voice is rough as he says, "Nice."

I step one high-heeled shoe out of my skirt and spread my legs for added stability. He leaves my panties on, and I brace myself with my hands flat on the desk right before he smacks my ass cheek. I hiss with pain as his palm connects, and he leaves a stinging spot on my bottom. The hiss transforms into a moan as he caresses the silky fabric over my throbbing flesh, soothing the ache.

"Is this what you want?"

My thoughts are foggy with desire, and I moan, "Yes...no."

He chuckles softly at my obvious uncertainty. "You need to learn a lesson."

Lesson? The only thing I need to learn is how his cock feels sliding inside me again.

He rubs the wet patch of silk across my pussy, causing a delightful tingle to course through me. I thrust my hips back, seeking his fingers. I'm already addicted to the feeling of him between my legs again, and I haven't even had his cock yet. He should have fired Bonny the moment he realized it meant he couldn't fuck me anymore.

When he presses his fingers down harder, I whimper and sway my hips, grinding against his hand.

"I think I'm learning my lesson really well," I purr at him. "I'm a quick study."

He laughs darkly. "Class hasn't even begun."

What is he talking about? I look over my shoulder at him the moment he spanks me again...hard. I yelp in shock and reach forward to grip the edge of his desk to prepare for more spanking.

He rains down slap after slap on my tender cheeks, and I'm lost in the painful pleasure as the world becomes hazy. I'm fast approaching the point where I'd do anything to please him.

My moans echo through the room, and when he strokes my pussy again, I'm frantic to come. I can feel the pleasure building in my core. Just a little more...

When I'm seconds away, he moves his hand and steps back so he can sit in his chair. I groan from displeasure. What's he doing? He needs to fuck me. Wait, I can ride him just as easily. I stand up and face him, resting my tender ass on the desk. I'm radiating with desire, and all I can think about is getting his cock inside me.

"Like I said, we need to talk."

His voice is surprisingly calm for a man who's sporting a massive hard-on through his slacks and a slight sheen of sweat on his forehead. Someone is worked up, and it's not just me.

"Mmm...less talk, more action," I coo and make another move towards the buttons on his shirt.

He clasps my wrists together and holds them firmly. "I'll tell you what's happening."

Why is he being difficult? I'll beg if I need to. I give him my most seductive smile. "You could tell me while you fuck me...I'm fantastic at taking *dick*-tation."

When his cock twitches and his jaw flexes, I know I've almost got him.

Before I can celebrate my win, he regains control and leans back in his chair, his eyes intense. "I wanted to bring you in here for an offer."

Oooh, an offer? "Okay. I'm listening."

When I relax and he can tell I won't pounce on him, he releases my wrists. Hopefully, this is an offer for his cock, or he'll have a cranky employee on his hands.

He pulls a business card from his desk drawer and hands it to me, and I study it, not comprehending what I'm looking at. It's a thick, black card with shimmering silver lettering. All the card says is "Plaything Resort," along with a phone number and email address.

"What is this?"

He smirks indulgently, and my pussy quivers with frustration.

"That's your Christmas gift from all the lawyers in the office, if you want it."

Can't he just be my Santa and I'll polish his North Pole?

"Okay, but what is it?"

"It's a weekend at a private sex resort where you can be a freeuse plaything for all the men there. Jon can go with you if he wants."

Wow. I look at the card again and a thrill runs through my veins like electricity from surprise and delight. Wait... I hesitate a moment, and I'm about to tell him that Jon wouldn't want to be used by a bunch of men for a weekend, but he seems to read my expression.

The corners of his mouth twitch. "Jon can watch. I know he likes that."

Mmm, yeah, my dear husband gets off on watching me be a massive whore. The thought of multiple guys at a freeuse resort using me makes my core heat, but I don't want to appear too eager.

"This is an interesting gift…"

Mr. Jacobs gives a self-satisfied smile. "Talk it over with Jon. If you still want to be fucked at work after you go, we can talk."

I want to argue that visiting the resort won't change my desire to be fucked by all our lawyers, but I keep quiet. I can play this game.

I slip the card into my bra and bend over to retrieve my skirt from the floor. "Okay, but I hope you realize what you're missing out on right now."

He caresses my ass after I stand up, and his voice is husky. "Believe me, Miranda. I know. But take a few weeks and think about whether you really want to start this up again."

His eyes seem to twinkle. "We might not be so easy on you this time now that we know what you're willing to do as a freeuse office toy."

Ooooh, fuck. Mr. King spilled the beans on all the filthy things I did for him back when I was his toy for the week before they hired Bonny. If I ever get to fuck him again, I'm going to give him a hard time about that, but I can't be too angry since it sounds like I'm going to get some thrills because of it.

"Yes, sir," I reply as I zip up my skirt. "I'll find out what Jon thinks about the resort."

I can feel Mr. Jacobs's gaze on me as I exit his office. As soon as I shut the door behind me, my body quakes with desire. Fuckity, fuck. I need a cock inside me, and now I have to work all afternoon while I'm turned on.

I take the business card out of my bra and study it. Hmm, if the resort is as lavish as this card is, this could be an exciting weekend. I'll have to see what Jon wants to do.

CHAPTER 3

Jon was all for a trip to the resort. We planned with Chris, the owner of the resort, to visit the weekend before Christmas. They had a cancellation, and I jumped at the chance. My pussy immediately got wet thinking of all the men I'm going to fuck. I even bought a new black bikini to wear in their hot tub and heated pool.

Chris talked to us about the resort and asked for our safewords. We also filled out forms about our sexual likes and dislikes. Jon will be at my side to watch over me, but it's nice to know the resort takes our safety and pleasure seriously.

After that, all I had to do was wait for the trip. The days crawled past and I got more and more turned on. Once Mr. Jacobs found out I was going to the resort, the lawyers at work started teasing me and brushing their fingers along my hand when I'd bring them paperwork. Those jerks knew exactly what they were doing.

I was getting a second dose of lust from home as well. Once I told Jon about the resort trip, we were fucking nonstop, every evening after work. He bent me over every surface in the house and made me beg, but then abruptly three days ago he stopped touching me and told me I'm not allowed to come until we're at the resort—the sadistic bastard. But that's why I love him.

It's fine. The day of the trip is finally here, and this hotwife is going to be stuffed full of cock soon. The resort is a few hours from our house, and I spend a large portion of the drive rubbing Jon through his jeans while he's behind the wheel. I'm trying to get him to pull the car over and fuck me before we get to the resort. It doesn't work. My man has learned restraint as he's aged, and he loves sexually tormenting me.

An hour into the drive, I bring up something we need to discuss before we get there and I'm trying to fit three cocks in my mouth. "Hon, you know what's going to happen this weekend, right?"

He blows me a kiss while still paying attention to the road. "Yes, my wife is finally getting her dirtiest gangbang fantasy fulfilled while I watch and count how many orgasms she has."

Whoa, he's going to keep track? That's hot.

I giggle. "Well, yes, that—but also, this is probably a once-in-a-lifetime opportunity. I'm going to embrace it and go wild."

Jon reaches over and squeezes my hand. "I wouldn't have it any other way, Kitten."

My heart flutters in my chest as a feeling of warmth steals over me. Yeah, I love my man.

I let my mind wander during the rest of the ride, and I suppress a giggle as I remember the Christmas party Jon threw for me a couple of years ago. This could be my chance for a do-over. I had a fantasy of having a train of twenty men on my ass, but I was afraid to actually go through with it. I've only had a few encounters with groups of men, the most notable being the conference room party with the four lawyers and then a crazy night when my husband's gaming buddies were over and I offered myself to them.

For the previous Christmas party, Jon set up this elaborate plan to make me believe that all of his friends were fucking me, when in reality, it was just him. He got me nice and subby by tying me up and making me wait. By the time the party started, I was in subspace and ready to believe anything he said. It was an amazing experience to realize at the end that Jon had orchestrated everything for me, but ever since then, I've been thinking about how I want the real thing. I want all the men's cum inside me. It may not be twenty guys this weekend, but I'm prepared to embrace a real gangbang.

As we pull up to the wrought-iron gates of the Plaything Resort, Jon rolls down the window and punches in the code the owner gave us into the keypad. The gates creak open, and he smiles at me.

"Kitten, you ready for this?"

I've been ready for this weekend from the moment Jon said he'd love to see me being a submissive slut for a bunch of men.

"Absolutely. I was made for this resort."

He places a warm hand on my leg and smiles. "You are. That's why I married you."

Oh God, as if. He didn't know how big of a slut I was until after we'd been married eight years—hell, I didn't even know—but the fact that he loves my dirty side is what's made our marriage so amazing all these years. Jon fucking me all over the house in response to the resort offer proves that maybe I need to keep fucking other men. I enjoy my possessive husband when he seems to be on a mission to prove that only he knows exactly how to please me.

I peek out the windows as he drives slowly down a long driveway to a gorgeous white house. There are tons of Christmas lights on the trees and bushes, but they're not currently turned on. I bet this place will look magical once it gets dark. I'm practically bouncing in my seat from a mixture of excitement and being horny. Jon chuckles at my enthusiasm as he parks the car next to an elaborate fountain in the middle of a circular driveway.

Before we get out, I lean across the console to kiss him and murmur, "Thank you for loving me, you big hornball, and thank you for allowing me to keep being your slut."

He takes advantage of my closeness and pulls me in for a deep kiss. As our tongues twine together, my core trembles with desire. Mmm, do I really need to fuck twenty guys when I have Jon for a husband? I rub his cock through his jeans again and moan as it pulses against my palm. Well, except he enjoys sharing me, and I've had more sex in the last two weeks than I've had in months. It's clear that my slutty ways benefit our marriage.

Our intimate moment is cut short when someone taps on the driver's side window. We pull apart, and I giggle when Jon groans. When I turn my attention to the man standing outside the car door, my body lights up with desire. Oooh, he's hot.

This guy is older, and he's wearing tight jeans and a snug T-shirt that showcases his muscular physique. He's in great shape for his age, and my mind conjures up images of him joining in on my gangbang fantasy.

Jon opens the door, and the guy introduces himself. "Welcome to the Plaything Resort. I'm Chris."

Oh shit, he's the owner. Bleh, he probably doesn't fuck the guests. What a waste. But hey, at least I'll get some delicious eye candy to enjoy while we check in.

I grab my purse and climb out of the car while Jon gets our luggage out of the trunk. I straighten my flowing red dress and try not to shiver because of the cold.

Chris approaches me, and his eyes twinkle. "I'm thrilled you both could make it during the holiday season. We go all out for Christmas."

I flirt a little as we follow him towards the house. "A bunch of orgasms is the best Christmas present."

Chris holds the door open for us and winks at me as I pass. "There are plenty of men here who would love to give you a gift."

Yeah, I'm willing to take all their "gifts" of cum. I wonder how many men I'm going to fuck this weekend. It better be more than five, since that's my current record. I want this weekend to be one that I'll remember forever.

As we follow Chris inside, he leads us to a cozy reception area where he hands me some papers. "I just need to see your ID and have you sign a few forms."

I take out my ID and hand it to him. Once he returns it, I sign the documents before letting Jon handle the rest of the check-in process. While Chris goes over the resort's amenities with Jon, I wander off to the magnificent Christmas tree in the corner with colorful ornaments and twinkling lights. There's also a little ceramic Christmas village set and wreaths and garland decorating the walls. It's charming, and I can't wait to explore the rest of the resort.

Chris calls out to me. "Miranda?"

I glance over my shoulder. "Hmm?"

"All the men know your safeword. There's no shame in using it if you need a break."

"Thank you."

I focus on the tree again and smile to myself. He doesn't know me. Super Slut Miranda this out this weekend, and I left Demure Miranda at home. I'm likely to take the twenty men all in a row and then ask for more. I doubt I'll use my safeword.

Two sexy, muscular, bare-chested guys walk in wearing shorts and sandals. Wait, bare-chested? It's not snowing, but it's chilly outside, so they must be freezing. I guess they could have been in the pool or hot tub, but they aren't wet, so I don't think that's the reason.

One guy picks up our luggage and carries it out of the lobby while the other man approaches me. My body instantly tingles as I grow more aroused. I'm in such a sexual haze at this point that I'd welcome this guy taking me right here, but I'm sure that isn't how it works.

Actually, how does this work?

The rule at the resort is that I can't ask the guys to fuck me, which is a bummer. With how wet and needy I am, I'd be going around and begging everyone to use me. I want to be a glorious mess by the time this is all said and done, and I'll enjoy every minute. I've given them free access to me while we're here unless I use my safeword, but it all depends on whether they want to fuck me. Oh shit, they better want to fuck me. How much would that suck?

I glance down at the guy's shorts and I can tell he's hard. Guess I don't have to worry about him not being interested, unless that isn't for me. The guy is in his prime and he's ripped. My fingers itch to trace the lines of his muscles on his abs.

When the man steps close to me, my eyes widen and my breath catches. Um, we haven't even finished checking in yet. He walks me backwards until I'm against the nearest wall. A delicious shudder shoots through my body as he takes my hands and pins them by the wrists above my head. He's massive, and he only needs to use one hand to keep me immobilized. I squirm, loving the sensation of being restrained and unable to escape.

My head swims with desire, and I don't know how to behave properly here. I don't want to screw it up and make him walk away, so I just watch him with hungry eyes and wait for him to do whatever he wants.

He explores my curves with his free hand, squeezing my breast roughly and making me moan. His gaze follows his hand as he checks me out. "Sexy," he says appreciatively. "Glad I won you."

Uh, he won me? I want to ask him what the hell he's talking about, but his fingers roam under the hem of my dress and I get distracted when he caresses my inner thigh. As his fingers inch closer and closer to my pussy, I can feel my panties growing more wet. Holy fuck, I need him to touch me.

When his fingers trace the edge of my panties, I press towards his hand, hoping he'll go for more. That earns me a sexy laugh, and he leans down to whisper in my ear, "I'm Tyler."

I smell a delicious cinnamon scent and want to lick his chest to see if he tastes as good as he smells.

"I'm Miranda," I say breathlessly. "Pleased to meet you."

I'm so turned on that my brain isn't working right. I'm barely able to stop myself from asking him to finger me.

His eyes crinkled with a smile. "You're not Miranda this weekend. This weekend you're our fucktoy plaything, and we'll call you whatever we want."

My face flushes, and I think about the questionnaire I answered before coming here. I said I enjoyed dirty talk and being called filthy names. I also stated I'm submissive, and I enjoy being tied up and spanked. The "our fucktoy" remark makes my core melt, and I can feel myself dropping into a submissive state. I'm dripping wet now, and my knees tremble. I've got a feeling that's the exact response he was aiming for.

When his fingers ease the lace of my panties aside, I have to remind myself to breathe as he explores my pussy. My stomach quivers when he nuzzles his mouth against my neck. His fingers spread my slick juices up to my clit, then circle it in agonizingly slow motions. I buck my hips in pleasure, wishing he was fingerfucking me—or better yet, had his cock inside me.

"Such a good slut," he whispers in my ear. "So turned on."

I moan softly as his fingers dip lower and plunge into my pussy. I whimper and shift my legs, spreading them further apart to give him easier access.

"Oh god," I gasp as he massages a pleasure point inside me and sends a zing of bliss through my core.

A small, amused chuckle rumbles from Tyler and he sounds proud of himself. I start to lose my grip on reality as the orgasm builds. I'm just a fucktoy this weekend, and I'll do whatever he wants.

I rock against his hand, seeking my release. Right when I'm on the edge of an orgasm, he slips his fingers out, and I whimper. No, he can't stop!

I'm dazed, and it's difficult to see straight while my body vibrates with need. When he brings his wet fingers to my lips, I immediately open them. I'll do anything he asks of me now that I've been teased by his magic fingers.

"Taste yourself," he orders as he slides his fingers in my mouth. "And clean them."

I swirl my tongue around his index and middle finger while he rocks them back and forth in my mouth like he's fingering a pussy. I taste myself as I enthusiastically bob my head as I clean him up. Mmm, I wish I could beg him to shove his dick down my throat instead. I've never been shy about my love of sucking cock, but I think that's too close to asking him to fuck me.

Tyler releases my wrists and pulls his fingers out of my mouth. When he steps back, I'm disappointed. Shit, I don't think he's going to fuck me yet.

He cups my chin, tipping my head up and forcing me to look him in the eye. "I'm done with you for now. Go to your cottage and know that at some point tonight, I'm going to take what I won."

There's that talk about winning me again. I'm about to ask him about it, but he slaps my breast hard and all thoughts drain from my head as I gasp from surprise and pleasure. Smacking my breasts was another thing I told them I liked. How closely will they follow my list?

With a knowing smirk, he walks away towards the rear of the house. My eyes follow him as he exits and I take deep breaths, trying to calm my racing heart and clear my head. That was...hot. I already have so many questions. Why didn't he fuck me? Am I a prize of sorts? If so, did he win my pussy for the night, or is it for the entire weekend?

Jon and Chris are both leaning against the counter, looking amused. Jon has a gleam in his eye and my face grows hot as I feel a little embarrassed about being such a thirsty slut before we've even made it out of the lobby. I said I was going to go wild, but I expected to unpack first.

Jon comes over and hugs me. "Come, my slutty wife, let's go to the cottage."

I laugh and give Chris a wave while he calls out, "Have a good time!"

CHAPTER 4

As I unpack my bags in the cozy, one-room cottage decorated for Christmas, I'm all aflutter from excitement. There's a small tree decorated in silver and red with multicolored lights, and it doesn't take long for me to get a feel for the space. There's a kitchenette with a dining area and the main room with a king-sized bed. The bathroom is the most impressive feature, designed for indulgence with a massive tub that can fit multiple people, as well as a separate spacious shower. I'm so getting Jon in that shower before the trip is over.

Jon's lounging on the bed, and it only takes a moment of indecision before I pounce on him and straddle him.

"Hey, whoa," he laughs and wraps his fingers around my hips. "What do you think you're doing?"

I fit my pussy against the hardness in his jeans and grind against him before giving him my sexiest smile. "Enjoying my vacation?"

I phrase it like a question, but we both know what I'm after. I want his cock.

Jon 'tsks' as if I'm misbehaving and thrusts his hips up to press his cock harder against my pussy. I moan as he controls my movements, making me rock against him faster. Jesus, if he keeps this up, I'm going to come.

When he bucks his hips and his cock rubs against my clit, my vision tunnels with pleasure. Just a little more pressure, and I'll climax. This is exactly what I was craving during the car ride down. Just a little more...

Jon abruptly pushes me off him, and I tumble onto the bed beside him with a pout. "Hey, I was almost there!"

He laughs. "Let's go check out the hot tub. I can fuck you whenever I want at home. This is my chance to see other guys use you."

I narrow my eyes at him and I want to protest that he can't just fuck me whenever he wants, but if I'm being honest with myself, he probably could. All he has to do is call me a good girl and tell me to kneel, and I turn into a needy, cock-hungry slut. Sometimes he teases me and makes me work for it by begging for his cock. Other times, he enjoys using me as if I'm his sex toy.

Occasionally, he lets me be in control, but that's not happening this weekend.

With a dramatic sigh to make it appear as though I'm not overly enthused with the idea, I get up and grab the black bikini from the dresser. I love that he wants me to get railed by other men instead of fucking me himself, but I don't want to be too eager. It's a fine line between panting over other guys' cocks while still making my husband know he's the love of my life. Not that I'm really fooling him. He knows exactly how turned on I am by the thought of a gangbang.

Jon finishes changing faster than I do, and as I bend over to put on the bottom bikini piece, he swats my ass as he walks by. I yelp from pleasure as he brings me my slip-on sandals.

"Don't take too long, my kinky Kitten."

I stick my tongue out at him as I slide the sandals on. There's no way in hell I'm walking to the hot tub in just my bikini, so I wrap a terry cloth bathrobe around me. Once I twist my long brown hair up in a messy topknot, I'm ready.

He's rummaging through our suitcase, and I can't help teasing him. "Geez, slowpoke! Let's go!"

When he turns around, one fist is closed, like he's got something in it. Uh-oh, what's he up to? I eye his hands suspiciously and he puts the thing in his hand into the pocket of his shorts.

Jon shrugs and closes the lid of the suitcase. "Ready"

Raising my eyebrow, I decide to let him have his secret for now. I'm sure I'll love whatever it is.

Since it's the end of fall, it's already getting dark, and as we step outside, I notice that someone has turned on the Christmas lights. The entire property glows like a fairytale wonderland, with colored lights on bushes, trees, and fences. I'm delighted and skip ahead of Jon, wanting to find the hot tub as soon as possible.

Jon and I walk through the light display, following a stone pathway to the center of the resort. As we get closer to the pool, the scent of chlorine gets stronger. They only allow one group of guests here at a time. That means if we encounter anyone, they are part of the resort crew and can use me. I'm trembling with lust at the thought, and as soon as the hot tub comes into view, my stomach drops when I see it's empty. Damn it, there's no one to fuck me.

I pause next to a patio table and remove my robe and sandals. Jon approaches me and rests his hands on my hips. I'm staring at the hot tub, feeling disappointed, when Jon gently nudges his erection against my ass, distracting me. Mmm, okay, so there might not be other people here, but I've got my husband to play with.

I place my hands on the patio table and bend over, grinding against him. What if he fucks me, and someone comes to watch? The idea is dirty, and I hope it happens. He takes a step back and uses his fingers to rub the fabric of my bikini bottoms against my pussy. I moan softly and my pulse speeds up, heating my blood.

We've been married long enough that I know how to get what I want. I wiggle my ass and look at him over my shoulder. "Sir, will you please fuck me?"

"Later," he replies, and then adds with a sly grin, "slut."

I sigh. Jesus Christ, someone needs to fuck me. He pulls me up and turns me around before lifting me and setting my ass on the metal table. I don't know what he's got planned, but I lean back, propping myself up on my elbows, and swing my legs while I bat my eyelashes at him.

"So what now, Daddy?"

He laughs at me calling him 'Daddy,' since it's not something I usually do, and he pushes my bikini top up, exposing my nipples to the cool air.

"Now, you're going to be a good girl while I do whatever I want to you."

My nipples harden from the cold, and he slaps one of my tits playfully. I giggle with surprise, and then moan from pleasure when he leans over me and sucks on the breast he just slapped. He tweaks the other nipple, and I run a hand through his hair while I close my eyes and enjoy the pulling sensation deep in my core. I can feel the wetness between my thighs increasing, and I might go insane if I don't orgasm soon.

His hand leaves my breast for a moment, and my eyes fly open when I feel something hard and cold touch my nipple. Jon stops sucking on my breast, and he's holding nipple clamps.

Oh, holy fuck.

"My Kitten needs some extra pleasure tonight," he murmurs while he opens the clamp and clips it onto my nipple.

I cry out from the sting, and he quickly puts the second one on. I rest back on my elbows again, and he stands between my legs and rubs my pussy through my bikini while the initial pain from the clamps dies down. Now it's just making me needier, though I know the real pain will come when he takes them off.

Just as my body tightens with need, the sound of masculine voices grabs my attention. I look down the path to where it leads to the main building and my heart races when I see a group of guys, which includes Tyler, coming towards us.

Three guys jump into the pool, and I shiver as I imagine how cold it will be when they get out. Tyler and two guys walk in our direction, and I whimper in need. I'm splayed out on the table with my tits out and nipple clamps on—not exactly how I thought I'd meet a group of guys for the first time. When Jon steps away, it's worse, and I fight the urge to cover myself. I feel like a sideshow attraction, but when my pussy gets wetter, I know I enjoy being the center of attention—especially since I look like a complete slut waiting to be used.

Jon sits in a chair close by as if he's settling in to watch a show. Yeah, I'm so about to get fucked, and I welcome it. When the men get close enough, I swing my legs again and try to pretend like nothing is out of the ordinary. I'm sure it's an everyday occurrence to have a woman in a bikini in the cold with her nipple-clamped tits hanging out.

Tyler smirks. "Looks like the slut is ready for us."

As they surround me, their collective gaze travels over my body, lingering on my breasts before moving down to my bikini-covered pussy. If there was enough lighting, they'd be able to see a damp patch on my bikini. I hope they're enjoying the view.

Tyler steps between my legs and trails his fingers over my pussy. I moan and wish the bikini fabric wasn't between us. Tyler pulls down his swim trunks, and I'm curious enough about what he's packing to lean up a little to get a good look. His cock is thick with an upward curve. Oh god, I want that in me.

When he slides my bikini bottom down part way, I lie back on the cold surface and lift my knees towards my chest to help him remove them. He grabs my ankles and looks at my feet, admiring the red polish on my toes.

"She's got pretty feet," one guy points out, and my slutty pussy clenches as if she just got complimented.

Oh god, I'm their freeuse toy to use. They don't even have to fuck my pussy if they don't want. My expression must have changed, because Tyler laughs and starts massaging my feet.

"Looks like the toy just figured out that we can do whatever we want to her."

One guy steps close and tugs on a nipple clamp, and I arch my back and cry out from bliss. No, no, no, they've got to fuck my pussy, right? What guy would have a wet pussy to use and choose to fuck something else instead?

One who wanted to prove his domination, that's who—because that's what I said got me turned on the most...being controlled.

The edges of my vision dim, and I shiver as a feeling of acceptance comes over me. If they don't want to fuck my pussy, I'll still enjoy every minute of being used. I came here wanting to be treated like a sex doll, and now everything I wrote down that I like might be used against me. They know I get off on being edged, despite hating it. They have all the tiny details of sex acts I prefer. Hell, they probably read that I enjoy having my feet rubbed since I put it down.

Tyler keeps my legs together and rests my feet over one of his shoulders. When he fits the head of his cock against my pussy, I almost laugh from joy.

He slams into me, straight to my core, and I writhe from ecstasy while he moans. "Lucky for this slut, I want her pussy."

As he thrusts into me, my whole body shudders as he massages the most sensitive spots deep inside me. It feels amazing, and I reach my arms above my head to hold on to the edge of the table and brace myself to let him pound into me harder.

One man plays with the nipple clamps while the other stands by my head and says, "Open that gorgeous mouth. It needs something in it."

I turn my head to obey, and he slides his cock between my lips. He's not as thick as Tyler, and I'm grateful for that while I'm in this position. His pre-cum is salty on my tongue, and I lick and suck for all I'm worth as the two men fuck me. I drift on a cloud of euphoria as every nerve ending in my body comes alive with the sensations of being taken. I love every moment of this, and I want more.

When the guy fucking my mouth suddenly pulls out, he sprays ropes of cum on my mouth and cheek. I moan in appreciation and lick my lips, savoring the flavor. Shit, he came before I did.

As soon as he's finished, the other guy takes his place, and I eagerly take him in my mouth. I close my eyes and just enjoy being holes for them to use. The new guy in my mouth has a slightly bitter taste, but it's not bad. I've swallowed my fair share of cum, enough to know that every guy tastes different.

Tyler continues to fuck me vigorously, and when he starts in with the dirty talk, my mind whirls.

"Fuck, I love the way your pussy milks my cock."

Mmmm, me too. I hum with appreciation.

"So good," he moans, and picks up his pace, fucking me so hard that the patio table shakes and creaks.

As he rides me, he growls, "I'm going to fill this pussy with so much cum, you're going to be dripping for days."

Shit, I wish that were true. Tension coils low in my belly as I feel my orgasm build. Why was I afraid of a gangbang? This is fucking fabulous.

Just as I'm on the brink of ecstasy, the guy in my mouth blows his load deep into my throat. He moans and shivers as multiple spurts fill my mouth, and I happily lick my lips when he pulls out.

"Such a cum dumpster whore," Tyler grunts as he keeps fucking me.

That's what I am. Just a vessel for their cum. I moan at the thought, and when Tyler whacks against me extra hard, I fall apart and scream as my orgasm hits me like a truck. All I see is twinkling lights as my body throbs from rapture.

"One," Jon calls out, and I giggle. I love that man.

Once I recover, I'm dimly aware of Tyler continuing to fuck me, but I'm too blissed out to pay attention to how his strokes change or what he's saying. It's not until a few minutes pass that my awareness snaps back into place when he stiffens.

Tyler groans as he thrusts balls deep, holding still. I whimper in approval, knowing he's pumping me full of his cum. Finally, he relaxes with a contented sigh and holds onto my legs, his breathing harsh.

"Alright boys," he declares. "I know I won control of the slut when I beat you at cards earlier, but I'm feeling generous. Line up and have at her."

My jaw drops in amazement. He really did win me.

The guys all laugh, and one of them grabs my arm. "She's facing the wrong way."

I blink with surprise as Tyler moves aside and two guys with wet hands pull me off the table. They evidently came out of the water. They turn me around and I see all six men gathered close by before they shove my head to the table. When the nipple clamps drag along the tabletop, I flinch from the pleasurable pain. Oh shit, I'm fucked.

One man stands behind me and runs his fingers along the curve of my butt. "Such a gorgeous ass. I wish I could fuck it."

Jon laughs. "Sorry guys, that hole is mine."

I recall a few years ago, at a BDSM event, when Jon's dominant side emerged, and in a possessive rage he said no one but him was allowed to fuck my ass ever again. No one has.

"Oh well," the guy says amiably. "I can fill her pussy with cum just as easily."

He holds onto my hips and thrusts into me so hard, I'm pushed against the table and the nipple clamps send a zing of pleasure straight to my clit.

"Fuck! Shit!" I cry out as he pounds into me.

He seizes my elbows, drawing them backwards, and he uses them like reins so I'm unable to stop my breasts from rubbing against the table as he fucks me. The bliss builds in layers, and I scream when I come once more, and it's so intense my eyes tear up.

The guy in my pussy only lasts two more thrusts before he groans and fills me.

"Two," Jon's voice rings out, and I have the insane urge to sob. I'm not sure how many orgasms like this I can handle.

Another man replaces him, and the sound of flesh slapping together echoes through the night as he fucks me. I barely recover from the previous climax when I'm coming again. This one is a full-body orgasm, and I convulse as lightning runs from the top of my head to my toes. I can feel my pussy fluttering and gripping onto the cock inside me, and my vision swims while the guy pounding my pussy finishes inside me.

I hear someone say, "Three," and I close my eyes, submitting to the moment. Everything hurts, but in a wonderfully exquisite way. I need these men to fuck me forever, and when the cock inside me slips out, I hear someone begging for more.

It's me.

I'm the one pleading for them to keep going as they swap positions and another man takes me. There are no words this time, just a cock thrusting into my pussy in a rapid-fire assault. In what feels like less than a minute, he's filling my pussy with cum and I shake as another orgasm crashes through me. I don't hear Jon call out the number. This time it's too much. There's so much pleasure running through my body, it feels like I'm a live wire as I tremble and moan. I sob incoherently as I plead for more while simultaneously begging for the torture to be done.

Someone turns me over and lays me on my back on the table again. I close my eyes, limp from joy as more men use me. I don't even know how many cocks are inside me, and at some point, someone shoves their dick in my mouth. It barely registers when he blows his load. He's got so much cum that it runs down my face when he pulls out.

I can feel the tension growing in my core again as someone fucks my pussy, and this time I can tell it's going to be a massive orgasm. I'm chanting out, "Oh god," as I hurtle towards ecstasy.

When someone removes a nipple clamp suddenly, I scream as the blood rushes to my nipple. I clench around the cock in my pussy, and the guy swears.

"Jesus, take the other off her," the guy fucking me demands, and I realize it's Tyler.

He hammers into me, and when the other nipple clamp comes off, the mixed pain and pleasure are too much. I explode and a surge of euphoria rips through my body so powerfully, all I can do is moan incoherently as it rolls on and on until the world around me dims.

I don't blank out, but I reach a point where it's just one continuous wave of rapture. Tyler finishes inside me, and when I hear a bunch of moaning but no one is fucking me, I try to focus and realize there's a circle jerk happening over me while each guy strokes himself.

I barely know what I'm doing as I open my mouth and stick out my tongue, hoping that someone can aim true. As cum shoots over my body, a spurt lands on my tongue, and I swallow it happily. I don't know how many loads hit me, but I can tell I'm going to be a sticky mess.

As I float in a sea of happiness, I hear murmuring, and then I feel weightless and realize Jon is carrying me back to the cottage. The air is chilly, and I'm naked, so I must have lost my bikini top at some point. Wrapping my arms around his neck, I rest my head on his shoulder and enjoy being taken care of.

I feel adrift as he carries me to the bathroom in our cottage, but I come back to earth when he sets me on my feet and hands me a bottle of water and a piece of string cheese.

"Drink and eat, Kitten. Then we'll get you cleaned up."

I devour the string cheese, not realizing how hungry I truly am until it touches my mouth. Jon removes his clothes while I'm eating and drinking, and he enters the shower with me when I'm finished. The warm spray rains down on me as Jon's soapy hands wash away the other guys' cum. Shivers run through me every time his fingers brush against my sensitive nipples.

After the shower, I'm relaxed but still flying high from the endorphins. I can tell Jon is very turned on by the way he's touching me everywhere and the sparkle in his eyes. As he dries me, I wrap my hand around his cock, enjoying the smooth softness of his skin on the steel rod underneath.

"Kitten, don't do that. You need rest."

I can hear the ache in his voice, and I tighten my grip on his cock and lift my gaze to his. "No, I need you."

That's all I need to say. He swoops down and kisses me passionately, sliding his tongue into my mouth like he owns me—which he does. He makes a soft moaning sound, and I squeak when he picks me up and carries me into the bedroom, his lips never leaving mine as we kiss with a fervor and desire that's all ours.

When Jon tosses me onto the bed, he's on top of me in seconds, pinning me down. I adore it when he manhandles me. I can be a dirty slut with other men, but only he gets all of me—body and soul.

Right now he's so horny, he doesn't want to make love to me. I eagerly spread my thighs wide as he slides inside me. He pounds me into the mattress, trying to prove he's better than all the other men. I love it when he fucks me like this. We surge together, and I'm surprised when I come quickly. My inner muscles clamp around him as pleasure rips through me.

"Ohhh, god," I cry out as the waves of bliss peak multiple times.

Jon grasps my hips and pulls me against him as he comes. As he fills me with his warm seed, he thrusts slowly, growling until he finishes. This man is all mine, and he knows it. I'll let him have me any time he wants, any which way he likes, and I love that he lets other men fuck me.

When he's finished unloading, he pulls out, and we cuddle together. As he holds me and strokes my hair, I'm surrounded by feelings of love and comfort. This is the man who loves me unconditionally, who gets aroused by the idea of men using me, and who wants me to come home afterward so he can have his cock in me and I can sleep contentedly with him by my side.

We kiss softly and whisper words of love, but I soon fall asleep in his arms.

CHAPTER 5

The next morning, I'm woken up by male voices in the kitchenette. Jon and Tyler are setting the table with covered dishes. I presume Tyler must have brought us room service. My stomach rumbles, and I can tell I'm going to enjoy breakfast.

I quickly dash to the bathroom to freshen up. Since we left my robe by the pool, I feel oddly vulnerable walking out naked in front of Tyler in the light of day. I'm digging around in the dresser for my nightgown when Tyler presses up against my ass and cups my breasts. They're still sore from the nipple clamps last night, and I moan as he pulls on them. Fuuuuck, that feels good. My pussy hums alive and I'm barely surprised when I find myself face-first against the closest wall with his cock sliding inside me from behind.

Movement from the doorway reveals Jon, who leans on the doorframe and watches us with an expression of amusement. He's casually stroking his cock through his jeans as he observes us, and he gives me a slow smile as I bounce against the wall, taking everything that Tyler gives me.

There's nothing subtle about this fuck, and Tyler pounds into me rapidly. I whimper in pleasure when he massages my clit. Oh god, I'm about to come. My head spins from the quick turnaround, from waking up to now being railed against a wall, but I embrace it.

As my inner walls tense up, he slows his fingers. I groan in frustration. Noooo! I'm so close.

"Beg for it," comes a voice that's not Tyler's. Jon is taking over, forcing me to accept his dominance.

"Please," I plead, squirming against Tyler, trying to get the stimulation back. "Sir, please let me come!"

Tyler resumes his circular motions on my clit, and I let out a throaty moan as it just fuels the fire building inside me. This is so dirty, with both men controlling my pleasure.

As I tremble from the oncoming climax, I wish it was Jon slamming into me. It's his touch I crave the most as the rest of the world fades away.

"Come for me," Jon demands, and Tyler increases the speed of his fingers on my clit.

My orgasm explodes, and my pussy flutters as a gush of wetness runs down my legs.

"Ohhhh, fuck," I cry out and press back against Tyler as every muscle in my body trembles.

Waves of pleasure pulse through me, radiating outward to the tips of my fingers and toes. This is amazing, yet I want something else, too.

I vaguely register Tyler roaring with release as he shivers and then goes still, but I'm focusing on Jon walking towards us, his cock glistening with his pre-cum. When Tyler pulls out of me, I immediately face Jon, kneel on the floor and part my lips as he feeds me his cock.

Sucking on my husband in front of Tyler is my way of demonstrating who owns me, but the truth is, I'm just a filthy whore who will do whatever I'm told right now. I'm in my element, and I'm living my best slut life.

As Jon rocks his hips, moving his cock in and out of my mouth, I think about the rest of the weekend. This isn't something I'm likely to experience again and I'm going to let this resort fulfill my deepest, darkest desires.

As I take my husband deeper into my throat, I glance up at him through my lashes, my expression filled with lust and neediness. I need more orgasms, but first, he needs to come for me.

Jon's movements grow more erratic as his breathing becomes shallower. He's fucking my mouth like it's my pussy. I tingle from enjoyment as he comes in my mouth. His hot, thick cum hits my tongue and I swallow it all. I'm a slut who knows how to please her man.

When Jon pulls out, I quickly swallow everything I can and then grin at him. My, "Good morning, my love," has a sing-song quality, and I can barely contain my laughter. Shit, what a way to start the morning.

Tyler touches my shoulder, and I turn around to face him. "Have a good breakfast." He winks at me.

He says goodbye to Jon before he leaves.

Jon helps me stand and pulls me in for a hug and a deep kiss. I sway a little and laugh. "I'm going to go clean up again."

He slaps my ass when I turn towards the bathroom. "Make it quick. The food is getting cold."

"Yes, Sir!"

I twitch my ass at him as I disappear into the bathroom.

I rub my belly through my nightgown after we finish breakfast. "Oh God, I can't eat another bite. What's on the agenda for today?"

He smiles mysteriously. "You'll see."

Hah, the jerk. I blow him a kiss. "Yes, Sir."

Jon cleans off the table and tells me to meet him outside in 10 minutes and to dress casually, so I decide on jeans and a tank top under a warm hoodie. If we're doing something outdoorsy, I want to be comfortable.

Plus, this way, if we run into a guy who wants to fuck me, he's going to have to work for it.

I wrap my hair with a tie to make a ponytail as I step outside. Jon examines my outfit, but remains silent. I fidget with the strings on my hoodie, wondering if it's appropriate for whatever he's got planned.

He takes my hand and leads me along the stone pathway around the center building of the resort. I feel confused, but willing to go with the flow as he guides me to a smaller building. When he opens the door, I see it's a recreation room... full of sexy, muscular men wearing nothing but Santa hats.

What sort of fucked up scenario is this? I try to count the men but get distracted by all the exposed cocks once I hit 10. My pussy hums and my nipples harden, and I almost laugh. Yeah, it doesn't matter what's going on. I'm a thousand percent down with whatever raunchy thing he has planned.

The men watch us as we enter. Some are playing pool, and some are at a card table with cards in their hands. I suddenly feel like I'm in a porno with a corny name, like "Here 'Comes' Santa Claus".

Jon holds my hand and pulls me over to a couch, but we don't sit down. He takes a cushion off of it and sets it on the floor.

"Kneel," he commands, and I obey without hesitation.

I look up at Jon with big eyes, waiting for more instructions. He picks up some rope off a side table that was hidden by the arm of the couch. When he ties my wrists behind my back, my vision goes fuzzy around the edges as I sink into submission. He knows exactly how to get me into subspace when he wants it, and I can tell I'm heading in that direction quickly.

"So, Kitten, here's what's going to happen."

Oooh, I get info! I perk up, and wiggle my ass in happiness and settle in, waiting for the explanation.

"A few years ago, I planned a holiday party for you..."

I nod eagerly, and he continues. "Today is for me, not you. This is my party."

I furrow my brow in confusion. Uh... what?

He leans in and presses his lips against mine before whispering into my ear, "I want to see how many Santas you'll blow before you say your safeword."

Ohhhhh. A shiver runs through me as Jon straightens up. Why is this so hot? He signals to the guys and they line up in front of me. As I open my mouth and a guy sticks his cock in, I give Jon the side-eye as he settles into a nearby loveseat.

This might be the most messed up thing Jon has ever asked me to do. I love it.

Well, if he wants to watch me blow some Santas, let's see if this slut can outlast the men. I focus on the dick in my mouth and try to bring him to climax as quickly as possible. That should send the message that this slut means business. I'm not saying I won't use my safeword, but I want to blow an impressive amount before I give in.

I want to see Jon's reaction. When my eyes dart over to him, he smirks like he can read my mind and knows I'm determined to swallow as many loads of cum as possible. I smile around the shaft in my mouth, giving it a little bit of suction and tongue action that makes the man grunt and thrust his hips.

Yep, that's the ticket. Come for me. I love how filthy this is. I'm just a cum dumpster slut.

The guy in my mouth groans as he spurts down my throat. As soon as he's done, another takes his place. I scoot forward while the new guy takes over my mouth. It's my train of twenty cocks, except instead of fucking my pussy, they're just fucking my face.

The current cock is nicely formed, and I lavish attention on it, sucking him deep and holding him there until I need to breathe. It doesn't take long for him to come, and after I swallow him down, another takes his spot.

I heat up quickly, and now I know why Jon was eyeing my outfit. He knew I was going to get warm. With my arms bound behind my back, there's nothing I can do but bob on every cock presented to me. The helpless feeling turns me on even more. My heart races with excitement as I get sloppier on this guy, and drool runs down my chin onto my hoodie.

After he comes, he pulls out, and the guy behind him laughs as he steps forward and tips my head back.

"Nice, slut."

It's Tyler. Hasn't he had his fill of me yet? When he slides his cock between my lips, I giggle. Guess not. When I taste myself on him, I shiver in pleasure. Okay, that's extra dirty. He didn't even shower after fucking me earlier.

As Tyler thrusts into my throat, he places a hand on the back of my head and twists his fingers around my ponytail, keeping me still so he can go deep. I've been conditioned to enjoy being used by now, and I moan while my pussy quivers.

Tyler's cock pops out of my mouth as he straightens up. He hasn't come yet, but someone else stands next to him and shoves his cock towards me. Well hell, okay, let's do this. I eagerly suck on him for a few minutes before he withdraws, and Tyler's cock returns to take his place.

I alternate between the two, anticipating the moment I get to swallow all their cum. It's interesting how different each man tastes and smells. It's more noticeable when you've got a string of cocks in a row, and I love the texture difference of each cock. Everyone is unique and I want to worship them all.

While Tyler slides in and out of my throat, I start to sweat. The front of my hoodie is soaked from all the saliva I keep losing. Am I supposed to tire of sucking cocks? I feel like I'm in my element, and the longer I stay on my knees, the more fun I'm having. I've never made so many men climax in such a short span of time.

Jon might think this blowjob party is for him, but I think he underestimated how big of a slut I am.

Tyler's thrusts speed up, and within moments I'm swallowing his load of cum. He pulls out and the other guy quickly shoves his cock into my mouth and explodes. Cum joins the saliva on my hoodie because I can't swallow it down fast enough.

I barely pay attention to who I'm blowing, and I'm lost in a sea of cocks. My eyes widen when I see the next one. It's thicker than any I've sucked so far, and I'm not sure I'll be able to fit it in my mouth. He enters me gently, allowing me to adjust, and I appreciate his consideration. If any cock was going to make me use my safeword, it would be this one.

He fucks my mouth slowly, and the rhythmic movement lulls me, and the world takes on a dreamlike quality. I no longer feel my body; I'm just a mouth for these men.

When he comes, it feels like it's never ending and streams of cum run down my chin. When he pulls out, I stick out my cum-coated tongue and wait for the next guy.

I lose track of how many men I've blown, but when it's Tyler in my mouth again, I wonder if I'm on a second round with everyone. Time loses all meaning, and I'm covered in cum and floating in my happy place as the men use me.

It could be hours or minutes when Jon calls out, "Okay, she's done."

Oooh, he called it. Does this mean I won? And what's my prize? There's no answer to the questions, and my mouth feels oddly empty as they all leave.

Once we're alone, Jon frees my hands and rubs my shoulders as I roll them. Everything feels good. He lifts me and sits with me on the loveseat, holding me in his lap.

"You're a beautiful mess."

He kisses my forehead, and I nestle into his chest, smelling his spicy aftershave that I adore. This is where I belong.

As I relax, my pussy throbs, reminding me I didn't get fucked. I wiggle against Jon, enjoying the feeling of his hardness. I bet I could dry hump him and come.

He groans. "Kitten, behave."

Does he even know me? I wiggle around some more and he kisses me softly before asking, "How are you?"

I know why he's checking. He needs to make sure I'm okay before he snaps and fucks me.

"I'm really, REALLY, good."

When I rock against his hardness, he laughs. "Yeah, you're good."

He lifts me off his lap, and when I stand up, I unzip my jeans and reach for his cock. He stops me and pulls his own pants down to free Rusty. I expect him to bend me over the couch, but he pushes me toward the pool table.

"Remember the last time I fucked you on a pool table?"

His voice is husky, and as he bends me over the side, I recall the day he fucked me at a friend's holiday party. Some guy walked past the doorway and saw us.

Jon pulls my jeans and panties down just far enough to fuck me. "Yes," I moan as he slides his cock inside me.

There's a slight soreness from being used so much, but that just makes it hotter. I wanted to leave this weekend the ultimate slut, and I'm getting my wish.

As he fucks me, I rub my clit. Between my slick fingers and his cock, I'm quickly soaring. When my orgasm hits, the intense pleasure makes me tremble as I buck my hips and push back against him as he fucks me through my climax.

Once I can tell he's about to come, I rock against him, urging him to finish faster. I'm desperate for him to fill me up—to prove that even though I'm a total slut, he still wants me.

He groans and I can feel his warm cum shooting deep inside me and joining all the other cum. When he pulls out, we both hastily pull up our pants before collapsing on the chair with me in his lap once more. He holds me close as he catches his breath, and I giggle.

"How many times did I come yesterday?" I ask as I close my eyes.

He snorts. "I lost track."

Yeah, I'm not surprised he doesn't know. It was a lot.

"Hey, what did I win for taking all those cocks?"

His laugh rumbles through his chest. "A lifetime of happiness with me."

I don't think there's anything I want more, but I playfully protest and swat his chest. "Bastard, that's not a win. That's just everyday life."

This might be the best vacation ever. We laugh together as I curl up against him and rub my cheek on his shoulder.

I peek up at him. "My love?"

"Yes, Kitten?"

His eyes glitter and I already see the answer in them before I ask my question.

"Do you still love me?"

As he gives me a huge smile, my heart beats faster, and my insides melt as he speaks the words I love to hear so much.

"Forever."

I twine my fingers with his and whisper, "Always," back at him.

We sit on the couch, holding each other as if we're in our own little bubble. I don't know if I want to fuck other guys today, and I know it doesn't matter whether I do, because everything I want is sitting here with me in my arms.

This is perfect. This is real, and this is everything.

The End

FreeUse Office Slut

Shared at the Office

Lacey Cross

Chapter 1

My loose black skirt swings around my knees as I stroll into work five minutes early. I can't remember the last time I was on time, let alone early, on a Monday. I was too excited to dawdle at home today, and I even skipped coffee.

Butterflies swirl in my stomach as I give Cindy a big smile. "Good morning. Isn't it a gorgeous day?"

Cindy looks at me like I've grown horns. "It's freezing outside...and it's a Monday...and we have to work for three more days before Christmas."

I laugh. "Exactly. Only three more days, and then we're off work until the New Year. It's a fabulous day."

Cindy raises her eyebrows, and I can tell she still thinks I'm crazy for being happy this early in the morning, but she doesn't say anything else as I head to my desk.

What Cindy doesn't know is that today is fabulous because there's a chance I'll get Mr. Jacobs' cock inside me. It's been almost two years since I fucked my bosses, and that's about to change. Slut Miranda is back in the building.

I drop my purse and lunch on my desk and perch on the edge of my chair as I log into my computer. I only plan on being at my desk long enough to message Mr. Jacobs and tell him I need to talk to him right now.

My hands tremble as I log into my work systems. The only reason I've got a shot at fucking Mr. Jacobs today is because they recently fired the office manager, Bonny, who's been cockblocking me since she started here. The last lawyer I fucked at work was Mr. King. I had a wonderful few days of being his freeuse toy, and then they hired Bonny. It was all over after that.

Now that Bonny is gone, everything's changed again. A couple of weeks ago, the lawyers gifted me with a weekend at a freeuse resort. Mr. Jacobs told me to think about whether I wanted to start back up with fucking them at work and to let him know after my trip. I got home from the resort last night, and I'm ready to lie on his desk and tell him to do me—okay, so let's be real here: I guess it's more like bend over his desk and beg to be spanked, but same difference, right?

When I finally get logged in, I send a quick instant message to Mr. Jacobs.

Miranda:

> Sir, I'd like to request a meeting with you ASAP.

That should be enough to get him interested. I can tell he's online, but he doesn't answer immediately. Shit, I'm going to have to be patient.

I spend about ten minutes pretending to go through my email inbox, but my body is tingling with anticipation and I'm barely reading anything. When the messenger flashes that he's responded, my heart leaps into my throat.

Mr. Jacobs:

> I'm free in 10 minutes.

Miranda

> Eager to begin, sir. I'll be there.

There's no way he could misinterpret what I'm wanting to 'meet' about. I don't normally tell him I'm eager for anything.

I lean back and daydream about walking into his office and immediately dropping my panties to the floor. That would get the message across. I wonder what he would do?

Giggling at myself, I glance at my computer, and the flash of my messenger app catches my eye.

Mr. Jacobs:

Meet us in the conference room instead of my office.

Uh...*meet us*?

Miranda:

Yes, sir.

My brain blips out, and I stare at my monitor, not seeing any of the words on the screen, while I consider his last message. What's going on in the conference room? I'm not sure I'm ready for what would happen if I walked in and dropped my panties for all four lawyers. Mmm, or am I? My slutty pussy buzzes as if she's trying to convince me otherwise.

Shit, fine, okay, Kinky Miranda wants it, even if Regular Miranda has some reservations. But it's not going to happen. My husband, Jon, said he's fine with me fucking my bosses, but a gangbang would need some discussion in advance, so there's no point in stewing over it.

A meeting with all of them is a good idea. I need to set some ground rules with them that include no ass stuff—especially for Mr. Parks. My heart races at the thought of Mr. Parks and his nimble fingers, which he's stuck in my ass before, and I flush with heat all the way to the tips of my toes as my pussy thrums in excitement. Jon has made it very clear that only he gets to fuck my ass, but I might need to find out if fingers are okay.

Shaking my head, I stand up and straighten my skirt. Enough fantasizing. I have a job to do, and if I don't have a cock in me by the end of the day, I'm going to be one unhappy Miranda.

I take the back hallways to the conference room to avoid Cindy. If she saw me, she'd pry and wonder why I had a meeting with all the lawyers.

She'd get cranky when I couldn't tell her anything. While I love the idea of my secret sex life starting up again with the bosses, it's not something to broadcast to my co-workers.

As I enter the large room, my mouth goes dry at the sight of all four men sitting on one side of the long wooden conference table. My gangbang over the weekend is forefront in my mind as I imagine what they would do to me right now if I begged them all to fuck me.

When they see me, they stop talking, but none of them rise to greet me. Their eyes linger on my curves, and I can feel my nipples harden as a slideshow of possible positions goes through my mind. Which one would fuck me from behind while I was blowing another? I'm a horny slut, and it wouldn't take much to get me to start begging.

Since I don't know exactly why I'm here, I decide to play it cool. I give a brief nod towards Mr. Jacobs. "Thank you for taking the time to speak with me."

Out of the corner of my eye, I see a slight smirk from Mr. Parks, and that expression alone makes me want to drop to my knees and crawl towards them. Just the possibility of fucking them again has turned me into a nympho—though it's probably the result of my wild weekend at the resort. I'm primed and ready for more sex.

As soon as we lock eyes, Mr. Jacobs responds. "Sit, Miranda."

He points to the chair across the table from where they're all sitting. Oooh, are they going to interrogate me? I can handle this.

When I sit down, Mr. Jacobs nods at me. "How was your little vacation?"

Little vacation? Hah! How do I respond to that? Should I tell him about how there was nothing little about all the massive cocks I had inside me? Probably not.

I settle on something vague. "It was very relaxing. Thank you all for the gift."

It's unsettling to be the center of attention when I'm uncertain exactly why I'm here. I scan the faces of the lawyers and pause when I reach Mr. King. His eyes bore into me, making me breathless, and I resist the urge to grind against my chair. I wish they would just rip my clothes off and take turns with me already, but it appears they didn't ask me here to fuck me...again, not that I would let them, but it still would have been nice if they had tried.

Goddamn, I'm a thirsty slut today. Jon is going to laugh his ass off when I tell him how horny I am. This is what happens when I'm offered the keys to the castle again. I might go crazy for a few days, but I'm sure my slutty side will calm down again.

I smile at the lawyers, acting like I'm unfazed, but I clench my hands together in my lap and tap my feet restlessly. They need to get to the point so we can discuss how and when they're going to fill my holes.

Instead, they remain silent as Mr. King places a tablet on the table in front of me and turns it on. Uh, what's going on?

A video starts playing on the tablet, and my eyes widen. Oh God, it's security footage of me sitting on this very conference table and fingering myself. I'm alone in the room, and the video has to be close to a year old. Can the earth swallow me up now? I'm flushed with embarrassment and lower my eyes as the recording plays out. I didn't expect a dose of humiliation to go along with this meeting.

No one says a word, and I can't stop myself from squirming under their gaze. My clit throbs with dark pleasure and it's difficult to focus on anything else. It's super fucked up how turned on I am right now.

After what seems like an eternity, Mr. Jacobs speaks. "We have at least four other videos like that of you around the office. What do you have to say for yourself?"

Do I apologize and offer to suck their cocks? I'm not sure what I should say, and I have no explanation for my actions...sometimes I get turned on at work, and I didn't know the cameras were on.

When I don't reply, Mr. Jacobs keeps talking in that firm, sexy voice of his that makes my stomach muscles quiver. "Why would a woman act like such a slut at work?"

I know he's not trying to slut shame me, and this is all part of whatever game he's playing. I look at him through my eyelashes while feigning innocence. "Well, maybe I was turned on?"

Or maybe I work with four sexy lawyers who were off limits and sometimes my fantasies got away from me. So yeah, it wasn't the smartest plan, but what're they going to do, fire me? We all know that's not happening.

A wicked grin crosses Mr. Jacobs' face, and I squirm as he speaks. "You're probably wondering why you're in the hot seat today."

I nod, my heart racing, and I can hardly focus on what he's saying. All I'm aware of is his mouth and tongue doing filthy things to me in my imagination. I need to get fucked so badly that my brain can't think properly.

"After firing Bonny, we had a long conversation, and we're not sure it's appropriate for us to engage in sexual behavior with any of our employees."

My mind freezes for a moment, and I suck in my breath. What?! Are these bastards messing with me? There's no way I've been cockteased by getting sent off to a weekend filled with nonstop fucking just to come back to find out they're being 'proper' about work.

He pauses, and I let out my breath. It doesn't register at first that I need to respond, so I continue to sit silently in my chair.

Finally, Mr. Jacobs asks, "Do you understand what this means, Miranda?"

It means they're going to have a mutiny on their hands soon. I almost snort at the idea of me going on strike due to lack of cock at work, but when I notice Mr. Daniels has a soft smile, it makes me relax. Oh god, they're just messing with me. I love and hate them when they tease me like this. It's time to flip the conversation in the direction I want it to go.

Blinking flirtatiously at Mr. Jacobs, I tilt my head and give him my best sultry tone of voice. "I think it means that I've been a bad girl who needs punished."

I can see that I'm getting to him. The corners of his lips twitch, and his tone is gruff. "And?"

I lick my lips while keeping my voice breathless. "Maybe I'm supposed to seduce all of you into fucking me again?"

Their gazes focus on me, and the attention makes my pulse beat rapidly. I feel like prey being hunted by four powerful beasts, and even though I should play hard to get, my pussy buzzes in delight. It takes every ounce of self-control to stop myself from laying all my cards out on the table and begging them to fuck me.

Mr. Jacobs chuckles as if he just thought of something. "No, you don't have to seduce us, but you do deserve punishment."

Mmm, now we're talking.

But before I can say anything, Mr. Jacobs continues. "Cindy is going on vacation after the holiday, and while she's gone, we want you to be our freeuse office slut. Can you handle that?"

My body tingles at how his voice becomes rougher as he's offering me my fantasy. There's no point in pretending I don't want this anymore.

I nod eagerly. "Yes."

He speaks firmly and makes the expectations clear. "For one week, you'll be available to us during normal work hours for whatever use we want. Your sole purpose will be to please us. You'll have a safeword that you can use at any point, and your continued employment here doesn't hinge upon you agreeing to any of this."

Is he saying that for the benefit of the cameras? I'm fairly certain I've made it obvious I'm down to fuck them all, and we've been doing this off and on for so many years there's no way I would assume my job depended on me sucking their dicks. I suppose he might want a record of this, though, so I don't push it and just nod in agreement.

Mr. Jacobs motions towards me. "Good girl. Now show us you're willing. Take your panties off and work the rest of the day without them."

An electric shock of lust runs through my body, and I don't hesitate before standing up and running my hands up my skirt to slide my panties off. I have to step out of my heels so I don't trip on them as I pick them up off the floor.

Dangling the scrap of black lace from my fingers, I purr at them. "Are you done with me? I've got work to do."

Mr. Daniels smiles outright, and the corners of Mr. Jacobs' lips twitch again as he says, "Yes, that will be all for now. No one will touch you until we're back from the holiday."

Well, that's a bummer. I can already feel my inner thighs getting damp, and it's going to be a long few days while I imagine what they're going to do to me.

"Of course, sir."

I start walking away, but Mr. King's voice stops me. "Miranda, we need a list of what we can't do to you and your safeword before Christmas."

Oooh right, I have things I have to tell them they can't do. "Yes, sir."

Mr. Daniels didn't speak during the meeting, and he's still smiling at me, so I ball up my panties and throw them at him. "Save those for me for later."

His grin widens as he catches them, and I spin on my heels and strut out of the room, making sure my hips sway as I walk. It feels like every inch of my skin is on fire and tingling with need.

At my desk, I look at the time. It's only 10:47AM. It's going to be a long two weeks until I get one of their cocks in me.

CHAPTER 2

Jon loves that my bosses are making me wait until after New Year's, and once I'm off work for the holidays, we have a wonderful and relaxing Christmas. Part of Jon's gift to me is a collection of new lingerie in a rainbow of colors. When he makes me model them for him, it turns into a wild fuckfest with him trying his hardest to give me more orgasms than I can count over the holidays. The prospect of me fucking my bosses again has revved his engine in a big way. I'm not complaining.

Despite how time seems to crawl, it's finally the Monday to return to work, and I'm freshly shaved everywhere and ready to be the freeuse office slut. I'm wearing a royal blue dress with a flowing skirt for easy access. I skipped panties, but I have on a garter belt with my favorite pair of silky black stockings with a seam down the back.

As I stroll across the parking lot and into work, my too-tall, strappy black heels click on the cement. I know I'm overdressed, but I look and feel sexy. No one but me and the lawyers are going to be in the office—even the paralegal is on vacation—and I shiver from the delicious unknown of how today is going to play out.

When I step through the door, I stop in surprise. Mr. King is sitting on a leather sofa in the waiting area. Huh, okay, I can make this work.

"Good morning," I purr as I stroll over to him.

Mr. King smiles as I get close. "You look beautiful. I'm going to enjoy taking that dress off you."

I flush at his compliment, and the dirty mental image of him removing my dress. I'm ready for him to take it off me this very second. I stand as close as I can to him, and his hand strokes my outer thigh, running along my silk stockings and up my dress. When he reaches the top lace edge of the stocking, he meets the bare flesh of my hip. His hand continues up, and I can see the recognition in his eyes when he realizes I don't have panties on.

"Eager this morning, I see. Naughty girl."

My breathing speeds up, and I'm practically vibrating with need. I daydreamed about one of them fucking me as soon as I walked in the door, but I didn't think it would actually happen. Now I'm not sure of anything.

As he caresses my upper thigh, his fingers mere inches from my pussy, my brain freezes, and I can't speak.

In a soft, but stern voice, Mr. King says, "It looks like someone is ready to be fucked. Sit on my lap with your back against me."

Oh yeah, I can do that. I drop my purse and lunch on the floor and do as he requests. I can feel his hard cock pressing against me through his pants as I settle down onto his lap. He wraps his arm around my stomach, holding me close to him, while his other hand inches my dress up. He caresses my inner thigh, and I spread my legs to give him better access. I moan when he cups my pussy with his big palm and grinds the heel of his hand against my clit.

Jesus, I barely walked in the door, and he's already driving me insane with lust. This is so hot. I love being the office slut, and Jon is going to enjoy this story tonight.

Mr. King's fingers dips between my folds, spreading my slickness around as he runs his fingers through my entrance and back up to my clit, circling and then moving away again. He's going to drive me insane if he keeps doing this.

I whimper as my head drops back on his shoulder and I tilt my hips forward to encourage his fingers to return to my clit. I'm rewarded with him circling my clit again, and I moan softly, encouraging him to continue as pleasure radiates from my core.

Holy fuck, where are the other lawyers? One of them could walk out here and see this. Pleasure ripples through me at the thought, and I almost giggle. Yeah, who am I kidding? I'd love it if one of them was watching.

It won't take me long to come at this rate, and every brush of Mr. King's fingers sends shivers of delight through me. When he slides two thick fingers inside me, I moan with satisfaction. I'd prefer his cock, but his fingers will do. He's rock hard underneath me, and I wiggle against him while he pumps his fingers in and out of my pussy.

Right before I come, he removes his fingers and pulls my dress down.

What the hell?

"You almost came, didn't you?"

I blink, trying to think clearly through the haze of lust. "Uh...Yes."

"I didn't tell you to come yet, my little freeuse slut," he says with a chuckle. "You only come when I tell you to. Understand?"

Fuck. I whimper as a sharp neediness overwhelms me. He better let me come today, or he's going to have one cranky administrative assistant on his hands.

He pushes me off his lap, and I straighten my skirt before picking up my purse and lunch from the floor. I'm uncertain what I should do and stand there awkwardly while my pussy tingles in protest of not being fucked.

"We're alone today. Everyone else is taking an extra day of vacation."

My eyes widen. Just him?

He continues. "I've got some conference call meetings. Get logged into your computer and come to my office in ten minutes. Be prepared to work," he warns as he rises from the couch and strides towards his office without looking at me.

Prepare to work? Does that mean sexy fun or regular work? Fuck, I guess I'll find out when I get to his office.

I head to my desk, horny and irritated. The jury is still out on how well I like him. He hasn't exactly been the friendliest over the last two years. Getting me all worked up to what I assumed was going to be an amazing orgasm and then stopping doesn't endear him to me.

If I had more time, I'd text Jon and whine. He'd enjoy knowing I'm a needy slut who isn't getting what she wants. Instead, I force myself to log into my computer before putting my purse and lunch away.

Nine minutes later, I'm walking towards Mr. King's office with a notepad and my favorite pen, determined to be a good assistant so he'll fuck me as a reward. His office door is open, and when he sees me, he gives me a charming smile. I take it as an invitation and slink into the room, rolling my hips so he can enjoy the view. I fondly remember being fucked over his desk that one glorious freeuse week, and my pussy is eager for a repeat performance.

He watches me with a sparkle of humor in his eye, like he can tell what I'm doing. "Are you ready to work?" he asks.

I really hope he doesn't mean actual work, but I'd gladly work on polishing his cock. I bat my eyelashes at him while setting down the notepad and pen on his desk.

"Ready to work, boss."

Mr. King gestures to one of the guest chairs in front of his desk. As I sit, I smooth the fabric of the dress along my thighs, and the motion causes his eyes to shift downward. He studies me, and I can tell he's thinking.

When his eyes roam back up, they linger on my breasts before focusing on my face again. I arch an eyebrow in response. He knows he wants to fuck me. He needs to just do it already.

After a minute of silence, I can't handle the suspense anymore and ask, "Is there something specific you want from me?"

Like...maybe your cock pounding inside me. Please?

Mr. King grin and rolls his chair back away from the desk. "I want you on your knees and under my desk. But first, take those ridiculous shoes off."

My brain doesn't know which part to respond to first. The idea of being under his desk is hot, but I choose to think about my shoes first.

I narrow my eyes and lift my leg, pointing the toe of my shoe at him. "These shoes aren't ridiculous." I'm careful to enunciate my words, and I sound argumentative. "They make my legs look amazing."

I pull my dress up to the top edge of my stockings as if to show him my legs and prove my point.

Mr. King responds with a heated gaze as he watches my every movement. "Yes, they do."

I give him a saucy pout.

He just sits there, studying me, before adding, "Now take your shoes off so you can service me properly."

My body buzzes at his words, and my skin flushes. Based on our brief time together, he knows I'm a submissive slut who loves being told what to do, but I'm also a bit of a brat. I stay seated and bend down to unbuckle the strap of one of my high heels.

"Slower," he orders in a gruff voice.

A rush of wetness dampens my thighs. God, it turns me on when he's controlling. I whimper as I go slower to please him.

Mr. King smiles. "Keep going, nice and slow, just like that."

All I can think of is dropping to my knees and sucking on him like the cock-hungry little whore he wants me to be.

Once both straps are loose, I lift one of my feet and remove my shoe, setting it down gently on the floor. Mr. King lets out a deep, sexy rumble of approval. For a guy who called my heels ridiculous, he's sure enjoying the show.

I slide off my other shoe, pausing for a moment before letting it fall to the carpet with a thud.

Mr. King leans forward. "Spread your legs. Show me your pussy."

Damn, he has no mercy, does he? I lift my dress and part my legs so he can see how soaked I am. I'm practically trembling as he leans back and studies me with appreciation.

"Now crawl over here and get under my desk. The meeting is about to start, and you're going to suck on me the entire time."

God, why is this so hot? I've had years of practice kneeling for Jon and other men, and I get out of my chair and drop gracefully to the floor. I crawl over to him slowly, making him wait. When I reach him, I only hesitate briefly before crawling under his desk. I'm a grown-ass woman, and it's going to be a tight fit under here. He pushes his chair in, effectively locking me between him and the back of his desk.

He spreads his legs, making room for me between them. "Now take out my cock and suck on it. I've got to get on this call."

Oooh, he's making a mistake. Does he not realize I'm going to do what-ever I can to make him moan? He better keep himself on mute.

I nestle between his legs and undo the button for his slacks. I lower his zipper so it's easier to release his stiff shaft and push down his boxers so they're out of my way. God, I want to suck on him.

I try not to show how impatient I am as I take out his magnificent cock and admire its length and girth. I want to worship his cock and learn exactly how he enjoys being touched, but today I've got to do what he wants, and I better behave.

I hear him connecting to the conference call, and after one quick lick to his velvety soft crown, I open wide to swallow him whole. Mmm, his heady musk sends my senses into overdrive, and I moan happily.

I slowly ease him deeper down my throat until he hits the back. Shit, he's too large for me to fit all of him into my mouth comfortably. After a few shallow bobs of my head to coat him with saliva, I try to suck down as much of him as I can.

He greets the people on the call, and I barely pay attention to what they're talking about. I have better things to focus on. With my tongue pressed against the underside of his shaft, I gag on his cock each time the tip slides into my throat.

I get into a pleasant rhythm as the call continues. Nothing makes me feel sluttier than being under my boss's desk while he's in the middle of a conference call. I feel a glow of satisfaction every time I hear quiet grunts or moans from him. I half hope the people on the call can hear him.

When I suck harder, he thrusts up to fuck my throat. Every noise he makes while trying to stay professional makes me giddy, and I take him down again. He speaks for a few minutes while I continue to suck on him. I have no idea how he's able to concentrate.

When he's done talking, he grips the side of my head with his hands and pushes himself as far as he can down my throat before pulling back while I cough and sputter.

Fucking A, Mr. King is one dirty, cocky lawyer. As if on cue, he thrusts again, this time angling himself so that he slides further down my throat. I try not to make any loud noises, but he's making it difficult.

Even though I hate him for making me gag while he's on a call, my body still thrills at the rough treatment. When he rocks his hips again, I look up at him and attempt to give him a death glare through the wood of the desk. Of course he can't see it, but I hope he feels it.

Him using my mouth like this pings a part of my brain that loves and hates being treated like a fucktoy. I could stop it with my safeword, but I don't want to. I want to feel like I'm just a hole to be used, and he's fulfilling that need superbly at the moment.

When he stops thrusting so far down my throat, I relax. Now that he's being gentler, I'm able to close my eyes and bob my head up and down, enjoying my thick lollipop.

My body trembles with desire while I suck on him and listen to him conducting business. I'm not sure how much longer I can keep this up. It turns me on too much to be used like this, and I desperately want to touch myself. God, I really hope he fucks me after the meeting.

Mr. King goes completely silent above me and holds his body taut. I pause with my mouth stuffed full of his dick as my throat works around him. Is the call almost over?

Right as I wonder if I should stop sucking on him, I feel a burst of wet heat hit the back of my throat. Holy fuck, did he really just come down my throat without warning?

I moan and swallow his offering as fast as I can. The thrill of drinking down his cum while he's on his work call has me tingling and warm with delight. I'm such a slut, and it feels incredible.

I swallow and finish licking him clean while he completes the meeting and signs off the call. When I notice him peek under the desk at me, I stop licking and grin up at him.

I expect him to praise me or give some sort of acknowledgment for being a wonderful office slut, but when he rolls his chair back, he motions me to climb out from under the desk. As I struggle to right myself, pushing up from the carpet, he stands, turning his back to me while fixing his clothes.

Without glancing behind him, he tosses out, "Go back to your desk until I want you again," over his shoulder as he exits his office.

What the fuck? That's it? Not even a thanks for letting me use your throat like a fleshlight? He needs to learn how to treat his freeuse office toys better. I grumble to myself as I put my heels back on and walk back to my desk.

And what's worse...how am I supposed to get any work done? I just want his cock in me.

Chapter 3

We spend the next couple of hours working, him off doing whatever legal stuff he normally does and me pretending to reply to emails. And by pretending, I mean me leaning back in my chair and listening to music while texting flirty messages to my husband to turn him on. I'm not totally sure Mr. King is going to let me come, so I need to have Jon primed and ready for me as soon as I get home.

When my work instant messenger flashes, I let out a tiny squeal in delight.

Mr. King:

> *I want you to strip and spend the rest of the day working naked.*

Uh...what? My body buzzes, and I can feel my inner thighs get even more slick at the thought. Oooh, this is fucked up and awesome, and such a perfect way to cap off the day! Jon's going to love this. Maybe I should take some pictures in the mirror. He might not believe I'm walking around naked otherwise.

Miranda:

> *On it, Sir.*

I pull my dress off and then mourn removing my stockings. Dammit, I'm sexy in these. Why can't I keep them on? Wait, would he spank me if I did? I know he's trying to mess with me, but so far, I love everything he's doing. If this level of fuckery continues with the other lawyers this week, I'll have the best job ever again.

I hold back a laugh as I spread my dress out on my chair so I can sit on it. Yeah, it's messed up that I have to sit on my dress, but I'm so damn wet there's no way I'm putting my bare pussy against the chair.

Now, how can I have fun with him? I'm definitely leaving the garter and stockings on in the hopes of that spanking.

Miranda:

> *I'm naked. Do you need any help with work?*

Hmm...that sounded pretty innocent, even if it was a lie and I'm not totally naked.

Mr. King:

> *Touch yourself until I tell you to stop.*

Miranda:

> *Yes, sir.*

It seems Mr. King is still in the mood to fuck me—or fuck with me—after all. I smirk at my computer screen. Two can play this game, sir, so bring it on.

I slide my hand down my stomach and spread my knees, giving my fingers access to my aching pussy. When my fingertips touch my clit, I can feel exactly how slick and soaked I am. I moan softly as I push my fingers inside my pussy and fuck myself. I need to figure out a way to convince him to let me orgasm today before I go crazy with lust.

I spread my legs as wide as possible and lean back in my chair. I close my eyes as I massage my clit with one hand and finger fuck myself with the other. Oh god, this is so hot. I imagine someone walking around the corner and seeing me fingering myself at my desk, and pleasure swirls in my core at the thought. Yeah, I found out I'm a fucking slut who loves being caught having sex after the night someone caught Jon fucking me on a pool table at a Christmas party. I remember how I felt when it happened and moan loudly, pumping my fingers into my pussy harder and faster.

I'm so busy I almost miss Mr. King's next message. Almost, but not quite.

Mr. King:

Stop touching yourself now.

Blah, just like him to ruin my fun. I whine to myself as I stop. My head is fuzzy, and I just want to come. He's successfully gotten me to where I would literally do anything he asked. I'd crawl on my hands and knees from my desk down the hall naked if he promised to fuck me.

Miranda:

I stopped.

Mr. King:

Good. Now I'm sending you a file and I need you to print it out and spiral bind it for me.

Uh...my head spins, and I try to focus on his words while my pussy flutters.

Mr. King:

Bring it to me when you're done.

Shit. Why does he insist on making me work today? This is starting to feel like two years ago when he made me watch the stupid training video and take a test.

Miranda:

Yes, sir. Printing and binding it now.

I take a minute to navigate to the correct page in our printing program, and I let out a groan of frustration when I see there are 96 pages total to print and spiral bind for him. Jesus, Mr. King, can I smack you now?

I give it a good ten minutes before I walk to the printer across the office. It's been a very long time since I've been naked and walking the halls, and this reminds me of the time I had my arms bound behind me and Mr. Knight was leading me to the conference room to fuck all the lawyers.

There's no way to erase all the memories of Mr. Knight, no matter how badly that ended, but at least I've got Mr. King to make new memories with—though the jury is still out on him. I liked him better earlier when I was sitting in his lap and I thought I was going to get fucked first thing in the morning.

My nipples are hard from the cool air, and it takes twice as long to spiral bind the papers as it normally does. I kept getting distracted by daydreaming of Mr. King coming in and fucking me over the counter in the supply room. That seems to be what he enjoys doing—he gives me a work assignment, and then he sneaks in and fucks me. So why isn't he here with his cock inside me yet?

When I'm finished, he still hasn't shown up, and I sigh in disappointment. Damn him. Guess I'll take it to him. When I stroll into his office, I drop the papers on his desk in front of him with a smile.

"All done, sir."

He gives me a stern look, one of disapproval. "I told you to be naked."

Oh, right. I give him my sexiest grin. "Oopsie. I thought you liked the stockings. Aren't they sexy?"

I lift my foot onto the chair in front of his desk and caress my thighs, as if trying to convince him I should keep them on.

With a slight shake of his head, he shoves his chair away from his desk and walks over to me. Before I can say anything, he's got me bent over the front of his desk. Ooooh, score! I wiggle my butt at him and give him a naughty smile over my shoulder. He rubs the soft skin of my ass, and I hum with pleasure. This is one of my favorite parts.

"I shouldn't spank you. You want it."

I don't deny his accusation.

I stick my ass back at him, daring him to take it, but then he slaps me. Hard.

Fuck, I love this part too, but then I whimper when I realize it's going to be a while before he fucks me. As I relax into the spanking, each smack sends a delicious wave of pleasure to my clit. Heat spreads over the tender flesh of my ass, and each spank hits that wonderful pleasure and pain point where I want him to go feral and pound into my pussy. I'll probably orgasm within minutes once he fucks me.

By the time he finishes, I'm a whining, desperate slut in need of a good fucking. I pant with need as pleasure spirals in my core.

"Get back to your desk."

Um...I look over my shoulder and blink at him, trying to focus through the haze of pleasure. Is he seriously not going to fuck me right now?

When he stares down at me, waiting, I huff and lay my head down against the cool surface of the desk. "Okay," I reply with another whimper. "I'll leave once the room stops spinning."

I'm actually fine to walk, but he doesn't know that. I close my eyes and drift for a moment until I hear him sit in one of the chairs behind me. Oooh fuck. I swear I can feel his gaze on my pussy as wetness drips down my inner thigh.

He clears his throat, his voice husky. "Tell me why you enjoy doing this."

I know exactly what he means, and he doesn't need to explain what "this" is.

"It's something Jon can't give me."

Which is true. Jon wouldn't make me crawl under a desk and suck on him while he was on a phone call. He enjoys edging me and teasing me, but there's a line he won't cross. Maybe he respects me too much, so it's not the same. I can't feel truly used when I know Jon loves me.

Mr. King stands up again and slides his fingers between my slick pussy lips to rub circles around my clit. "Can't? Or won't?"

"Oooooh, god. Does it matter?" I moan and push back against his hand, trying to get him to slide a finger inside me.

He pulls his hand back and, before I can complain, slaps my pussy. I cry out as sharp pleasure ripples from my pussy.

"I asked you a question, slut. Can't, or won't?"

He slaps my pussy a few more times, and I pant out, "Can't—he can't. He's a soft dom. He can't give it to me as hard as I need."

I almost feel like a traitor admitting this to Mr. King, but Jon and I have talked about it many times over the years. We found a very satisfying middle ground for both of us. I've never doubted how much he loves me, so it works, but sometimes I crave more, and I'm so fucking lucky that Jon gets off on sharing me so I can get that part of me satisfied elsewhere.

Instead of slapping my pussy again, Mr. King puts his fingers back on my clit and continues to tease me. This time, though, I'm starting to think he's not planning to fuck me at all. The shitty and wonderful thing about that is I'd be okay if he doesn't. I love the angst of not getting fucked when I want it.

"Are you a masochist, Miranda?"

His words take me out of the moment for a bit, and I look up at him in confusion. "What?"

He rubs my clit again, and the pleasure causes me to jerk my hips towards his hand for more as he repeats himself. "Are you a masochist?"

I think for a moment while I continue to enjoy him circling my clit. "No, I'm just a slut who likes to be used."

Mr. King laughs darkly. "Well, I agree with you on that."

As if to prove the point, he thrusts two of his fingers into my pussy, curling them to massage the pleasure point inside me as he begins to roughly pump them in and out. I gasp at how quickly my arousal peaks, and I'm on the verge of an orgasm within seconds. I cry out, trying to stifle the sound by burying my face in my arm as I force myself not to come. Oh fuuuuck. I don't know if I can stop it.

I'm trembling and on the edge as he pulls his fingers out. I hear the rustle of his clothes a moment before he slams his cock into me.

"Ohhh, god!" I cry out and arch my back as he pushes inside me to the hilt and sets a punishing rhythm, fucking me with long, hard strokes.

"Please, let me come, sir. Please?"

It's pure torture not being able to come, but Mr. King makes no sign of giving me relief. I squeeze down on his cock, and tendrils of pleasure shoot to my core, making it worse. I'm afraid my brain is going to melt from pleasure before he lets me come.

When he abruptly pulls out, I tremble with the effort of holding back an orgasm and mewl at the loss of his cock.

I'm panting, lost to the madness of needing to come. I whine pathetically as I plead with him, "Don't stop. Oh god, don't stop."

Mr. King chuckles as if my desperation amuses him before sinking back into my swollen pussy with a single stroke. When his fingers find my clit, rubbing, circling, and massaging, I can't hold back any longer. My orgasm tears through me with the ferocity of an electric charge, causing all my muscles to lock and spasm and making my lungs seize up so that I can't breathe.

Mr. King's continues to pound into me, extending one of the most powerful orgasms I've had in the last week. Shit, this rivals all the orgasms I had at the freeuse resort.

When my body relaxes, he moves his hand from my clit and lifts me up. His cock is still inside me as he sits down on a chair with me in his lap, his chest pressed against my back. He's still clothed, other than having his cock out, and I can feel his warmth through his dress shirt.

"Now stay still so I can use you like a cum dumpster whore."

It takes me a moment to focus on the present, and I don't reply as he moves my hips like I'm a sex doll that he's trying to get off with. His sheer size overwhelms me into submission, and I'm more than happy to be his fucktoy and just sit here, impaled on his glorious cock.

He runs his hands over my curves possessively, squeezing and pinching wherever he wants. I whimper but don't complain because I love how he's treating me. God, he makes me feel like his slut. When his fingers graze my sensitive clit, I suck in a sharp breath as I feel another orgasm building.

While he pinches and squeezes my clit, I throw my head back to rest against his shoulder and whimper. Pleasure ripples up and down my spine, and I do my best to hold still as another orgasm rips through my body. My pussy flutters and squeezes his cock in response to the ecstasy rocketing through me.

This time Mr. King groans with pleasure when he feels me coming on his cock, but he doesn't relent. While my pussy still throbs, he wraps his arm around my waist, keeping me immobile as he thrusts his hips up, pounding my pussy until his strokes become jerky. He comes with a deep groan of satisfaction as I feel his warmth flood my pussy.

We're both silent and still for several minutes, basking in our afterglow before Mr. King helps me up off his lap. He holds me in his arms, making sure I'm steady. When he kisses my forehead, I get the sense that he's not as rough as he'd like me to think.

As if he can read my thoughts, he tells me, "Now get back to work, slut. No clothes until you leave. And make sure you eat and drink something."

I can't stop myself from grinning. "Yes, sir!"

It's only when I settle down at my desk again that I think about how I feel about him. There's a connection between us, even though we haven't spoken much at all since he joined the firm. We have a sexual chemistry that is unlike anything I've ever experienced with any of the other lawyers before. Back when Mr. Knight was here, he was more of a mentor and teaching me about submission, but Mr. King just enjoys using me with no strings attached. He's not trying to be my friend. It's perfect.

I eat a snack and hydrate as I try to answer the same work emails that I've been needing to reply to all day. I can feel his cum leaking out of me onto the dress I'm sitting on. Fuck, that's dirty.

Oh shit, I never took the naked picture for Jon. I open up the camera on my phone, angle it to show him exactly how dirty and used I look, and snap a pic before forwarding it to my husband with a simple message.

Miranda:

> Fucked on my boss's desk with his cum running down my legs. Do you want me to shower when I get home?

Mr. King may be a bastard for playing with my emotions like he did, but I really do enjoy being his dirty office slut, and I can't wait for what the other lawyers are going to do to me tomorrow.

It only takes my husband a few minutes to text back.

Jon:

> Nope. You need more cum in you before you shower.

Yeah, he knows what I like. I send him a heart emoji and try to buckle down and concentrate on the emails. After a few minutes, I give up and daydream about fucking Jon. When it's time to leave, I slide my dress on, and I'm adjusting it as Mr. King comes by my desk.

"Mr. Jacobs said to tell you to wear your pink shirt tomorrow."

My mouth drops open, and my pussy buzzes at the thought of them discussing me.

I nod. "Yes, sir. Have a good evening."

He says goodnight to me as I gather my purse and lunch sack. I get into my car with a dazed smile on my face and hurry home to get fucked by

Jon. I'm almost as eager to tell him all about Mr. King as I am to feel my husband's cock inside me.

CHAPTER 4

I'm a good girl and don't shower. I'm sitting on the kitchen table when Jon gets home. The only clothes I'm wearing are my garter belt and silk stockings. I've got my feet resting on separate chairs, and I'm spread wide open. I've been playing with myself while I wait for him, and my pussy is swollen and wet.

His eyes glaze over with lust as he sets his lunch and water bottle on the counter.

"So tell me..." His voice is low, and it sends a shiver of pleasure straight to my core. "How much of a filthy slut were you today?"

I swirl my fingers around my clit and moan, "Mmm, so dirty."

This is the game we play, and I enjoy making him work for all the details after I fuck someone else.

Jon starts removing his clothes, and I vibrate with need. As he pulls off his shirt, he asks, "What did Mr. King do?"

I slide my fingers over my pussy as I talk, stroking and circling my clit with delicate movements, and I watch Jon undress the rest of the way. I'm ready to pull him on top of me the moment he's naked.

"I crawled under his desk and sucked on him while he was on a call."

Jon kicks his pants to the side and moves between my legs. His cock is hard and would slide in so easily. I reach forward to rub his shaft slowly. I want him to be as desperate as I am.

"Did he let you come?" he asks in a hoarse whisper.

I circle the tip of his cock with my thumb, spreading the pre-cum like it's lube. I relish the little shudder that I feel rippling through him.

"Eventually," I admit. I grin wickedly. "He made me come when he bent me over his desk."

Jon groans as I guide his cock to my pussy. As soon as the head slides in, Jon takes over. He sinks inside me balls deep, and I grip his shoulders as he fucks me leisurely. Shit, where is my crazy, worked up husband who was supposed to fuck me hard?

My head spins from the slow pace he's setting, and I wrap my legs around his waist and squeeze tightly. Jon grunts but continues to move in and out at an infuriatingly slow rate. What the hell is going on?

After a minute, he leans in close, putting his cheek to mine before whispering in my ear, "How does it feel to have two men decide when to allow you an orgasm?"

A rush of pleasure zings straight into my brain at his words. Shit. I raise an eyebrow at him and tease, "I don't know, I could do this all night. How about you?"

With a wolfish grin, Jon rears back and slams into me hard, bottoming out. "Game on."

A strangled cry leaves me, and I throw my head back in shock and delight. Fuck yes. I thought he was going to make me beg, but this is so much better. When he slams into me again, my eyes roll back as a thrill shoots through me. Yes, oh god, this is exactly what I need.

For several moments, neither of us speaks, and all I can hear is the sound of our moans and the creak of the table. Jon fucks me like a man on a mission, and I cling to him as I meet him thrust for thrust. A tingling sensation starts in my toes, traveling up my legs and settling in my stomach.

It radiates outward, sparking tiny explosions along the way. My body tenses as it climbs higher. Just before I'm thrown over the edge, Jon pauses mid stroke.

Our eyes lock together as I hover there with his cock buried deep in my cunt.

"No!" I whimper as he shifts back, leaving just the tip of his cock inside me. "Jon!" I try to push against him with my heels, but his hands on my knees keep my legs locked apart.

"Patience, kitten."

He winks, and I whimper with frustration. I'm quivering with lust as I reach up and twist one of my nipples. I can't just lie here like this without coming. I'm about half ready to climb off this table and push him on the floor to ride him.

When he notices what I'm doing with my hand, Jon shakes his head. "Naughty, naughty, kitten."

Grasping my hand, he pins it down against the table next to me before leaning down to suck my other nipple into his mouth. I writhe under him, wishing he was pounding me back into the orgasm I was so close to.

When he switches breasts, taking the other one in his mouth, I wiggle, trying to get friction from his abdomen touching my pussy. I love my husband dearly, and he knows exactly how much teasing I can take. And the best thing about him is that he always delivers on the build-up and makes it worth the wait.

"Do you think you deserve to come again today?" Jon whispers in between gentle nibbles to my breast.

I squeal out, "Yes! Now, can you please fuck me? Please?"

I'm so desperate for release that I can barely see straight.

"Knees together," he orders gruffly, pressing them together with his hands. I leave them that way, pulling them close to my torso to tempt him.

He murmurs, "Good girl," as he slides back inside me. My head spins from the praise, and I shudder at the joy of him filling me.

I grab for the edges of the table so I can brace myself as he fucks me wildly, thrusting like a machine. I close my eyes and let the pleasure wash over me. A rush of euphoria roars through me, and I explode all over his cock.

My moans are just one long cry of pleasure as he fucks me through my orgasm. Tilting my head back, I allow myself to experience every raw emotion racing through me. When he comes, he joins me with a growl, burying himself completely and filling me with his cum.

My mind goes blank from pleasure, and when I come back to awareness, Jon is looking down at me with a wide, satisfied smile. "I'm not done with you tonight, slut. But first we're going to shower and eat."

I nod eagerly.

He continues. "And then you're going to tell me every single detail of today while I fuck you again, but this time, you aren't coming."

Oh god, that's mean. I love it.

I lower my legs, and he pulls me up and kisses me deeply. As our tongues twirl, I think about how much of a needy slut I'm going to be at work tomorrow if I don't come again tonight.

Jon might be a soft dom who can't fuck me as rough as I want that often, but he sure knows how to fuck with my mind in the most delicious ways.

This is going to be a fun week.

The End

Freeuse Office Games

Games

A Hotwife Shared

Lacey Cross

CHAPTER 1

I practically float through the office doors, my mind replaying yesterday's events on a loop. My body tingles at the memory of Mr. King using me and driving me crazy. I really hope no one expects me to do actual work today. I'm revved up and ready for more playtime.

The receptionist, Cindy, is on vacation, and the office is quieter than usual. Which is good, considering I'm the designated entertainment for four very sexy lawyers this week. The thought makes me squirm as I settle into my chair, smoothing down my pink button-down shirt.

Jon chose my outfit this morning, keeping in mind Mr. Jacobs' request yesterday that I wear my pink shirt. To go with it, my husband selected a white lace bra and panty set that he said would blow my boss's mind, along with a short black skirt and spiked high heels. Before I left, he kissed me and told me to "Be a good slut for your bosses today." I'm not sure what I did in a past life to deserve Jon in this one, but it must have been something fabulous.

I'm logging into my computer programs when the instant messenger pings. My heart jumps into my throat when I see who it's from.

Mr. Jacobs:

Come to my office. Now.

Oh god–Mr. Jacobs is the senior partner at my law firm, and I love it when he gets demanding—especially knowing this might lead to something deliciously inappropriate that includes multiple HR violations. My spiked heels make me feel sexy and I put an extra swing into my hips as I make my way into his office. He's sitting behind his desk, devastatingly handsome in a charcoal suit. My mind flashes to previous times where his pristine suit was significantly rumpled when I left his office. It's been way too long since he's spanked me, and I think it's time to change that.

"Leave the door open. You won't be here long." His voice sends shivers down my spine. Dammit. I wanted the door closed.

He hands me a stack of papers. "These need to be completed within the hour. Miss one, and you'll find yourself back in here and bent over my desk."

My pussy clenches at his words. I scan the list on the top page, trying to focus despite the wetness growing between my legs. What the heck? I'm not in the mood to deal with my job today. He needs to rethink this plan.

"What if..." I pause, and give a sassy smile. "What if I want to be over your desk?"

"Let me be clear," he rumbles with authority, "your chance for an orgasm today depends entirely on your job performance. Understand?"

My pulse quickens. Oooh, stern Daddy Jacobs is out. Challenge accepted.

Lowering my lashes, I give him my best cutesy and contrite, "Yes, Mr. Jacobs," even though we both know I'm probably not going to do any of this paperwork. I'm sure he doesn't actually expect me to.

I rush back to my desk, but my mind refuses to cooperate. I'm too busy daydreaming about the past and remembering how much I loved being spanked by Mr. Jacobs–the heat that radiated from his palm, the lingering sting, the anticipation as I waited for the next strike. Also...each time I finish one task, the pile seems to multiply. I swear it's breeding.

I'm not even halfway through the pile when the hour is up. My stomach flutters with excitement as I wait for his summons. When my instant messenger flashes, I expect him to ask me about the forms, but he doesn't.

Mr. Jacobs:

> *Please set up the conference room and get coffee ready for the attendees.*

Ugh. This is bullshit. My mind races as I do as I'm told. Where's my spanking for not finishing the forms? I'm the freeuse office slut. I was supposed to have four cocks inside me by now. After Mr. King fucked me all over the office yesterday and made me suck him off under his desk, I expected more today. I think the bastard is teasing me and making me wait for it.

My hands shake as I fill the coffee carafe and arrange the cups. I'm so turned on, I can barely think straight. As I'm finishing up, Mr. Jacobs comes in with a stack of papers and empty manila folders.

He closes the door behind him. "Miranda, you're crawling at a snail's pace today. You should be done by now."

I open my mouth to tell him that maybe if he had spanked me, I would have picked up the pace, but I quickly close it again. Yeah, probably not. I would have just wanted more.

I raise an eyebrow at him while he separates the papers into three piles and sets the empty folders next to them on the table. "Each folder needs one of each form before the meeting starts. You have 10 minutes."

There wasn't a meeting on the calendar, and organizing folders this way definitely isn't how things are done around here. This is a set up if I ever saw one–and I'm okay with that.

He doesn't move away from the table and I have to crowd close to him to reach the forms. Daddy Jacobs is being a bit of a jerk, and with how wet my panties are, my slutty pussy loves it.

I quickly start filling the folders, but him watching over me is making me feel clumsy and I keep accidentally grabbing multiple sheets from the same pile. I'm about to snap at him and ask him if he doesn't have something better to do when he suddenly moves in behind me and unzips my skirt. Ohhh, hello.

My skirt pools at my feet and he rubs his hands over my panties. My pink button-down shirt had been tucked in, but now the ends trail down my stomach and ass. From where he's standing, I bet my legs look amazing in these heels.

When he rubs my pussy, I purposely jut my ass out towards him and his attention makes me inadvertently slow my hand movements.

"How long has it been since I fucked you?" he growls as he continues to run his fingers over the fabric covering my pussy.

"Two years," I breathe out softly. Most of our previous fun times at the office started with a punishment spanking that lead to sex. What he's doing now leaves me uncertain what to expect.

His hand lands on my ass in a sharp spank, and I gasp. Yeah, never mind, there it is.

"That's for being such a tease the last two years when you knew I couldn't fuck you."

Ooooh, god. What the hell? It's not my fault he couldn't fuck me. I'm not the one who hired Bonny, which turned out to be the demise of our office fuckfest. Since he's the senior partner, he would have had a lot of sway in their choice for office manager. Maybe HE should have thought of that when making the final decision. I moan when he spanks me again.

"Keep working," he says gruffly.

Fuck, okay. Must concentrate...Mr. Jacobs' spanks fall in a hypnotic rhythm, making it impossible to think straight. Each one sends jolts of delight through my body. I'm torn between the need to complete the folders and the overwhelming desire to close my eyes and bliss out. I'll just get them done quickly. My hands move on autopilot, shoving papers together.

"Time's running out," he warns as he delivers another painful spank.

When he pulls my panties down to my knees, I bite back a groan and grip the edge of the table. He slides a finger into my pussy and fucks me with it as pleasure swirls in my core. Um, how long have we been in here? Are people about to walk in?

He stops finger fucking me and I hear the sound of his zipper as the teeth slowly part. Every nerve ending sparks alive as the tip of his cock gently probes my pussy. Mmm, now this is more like it.

He grasps my hips firmly, his fingers digging into my flesh. I welcome the slight pain when he slowly sinks into me. Holy fuck, I forgot how much I love his cock after having gone so long without it.

He pauses once he bottoms out and I realize my hands have gone still. Oops, shit. I quickly start stuffing files again as delight ripples through me.

Mr. Jacobs pins my hips against the table with every slow thrust. It's almost impossible to concentrate. Although I'm hindered by my panties, I spread my legs as wide as I can to encourage him to fuck me harder, but he doesn't. Each drag of his cock along the sensitive nerve endings inside me makes my head spin and it doesn't take long for me to feel like I'm losing my mind from pleasure.

"The conference starts any minute now and you're only halfway done. I'm not rewarding your poor work ethic with an orgasm," he taunts me as he slaps my ass.

Ugh. What a jerk. I try to shuffle the pages again. Wait, where was I?

When he moves his hand around to my front and fingers my clit, I roll my hips and let out a small involuntary whimper. Oh fuck. My hands tremble as I haphazardly shove forms into the last few folders. I'm not even paying attention anymore to what I'm putting into each one.

When he sees I'm done with my task, he speeds up his thrusts. I try to hold back my orgasm as the delight builds. The tip of his cock hammers against the magical spot deep inside me, and the pleasure is so intense, I'm going to come at any moment.

A knock at the door shatters my concentration, and I let out an embarrassingly loud groan.

"The clients are here," Mr. Parks calls through the door.

Mr. Jacobs slams into me one last time and groans as he explodes. His warm cum coats my inner walls as he unloads. Ohhhh, no, what? It can't be over.

He jerks against me, unloading ropes of cum before pulling out. I slump down onto the table, squeezing my eyes closed for a moment as I feel his cum leak out of me and drip down my leg. Today really isn't going how I expected. I thought I'd have come at least once by now.

I'm in a daze as I watch him move to a side table and pick up a container of wet wipes I didn't notice before. They aren't usually in here. He was prepared.

As he cleans himself up, he says, casually, "You better make yourself presentable before everyone walks in here."

Fuck, shit. I hastily pull my panties and skirt up, tucking my blouse back in. Mr. Jacobs walks back over to me and whispers in my ear, "I'm not done with you. Go be a good slut and earn your paycheck for the next hour."

He spanks me and I yelp. My legs feel like jelly as I leave. I run into Mr. Parks escorting four other lawyers down the hall. Oh god, is my hair a mess? Heat blooms across my cheeks as I realize my skirt isn't on straight.

Mr. Parks gives me a devilish smile as they pass, and I wish the floor would open up and swallow me, even as a zing of naughty delight turns me on even more. When I reach my desk, I plop down into my seat and feel Mr. Jacobs' cum leaking into my panties. This is messed up in the best of ways.

Instead of tackling my to-do list, I grab my phone from my purse and text my husband.

Miranda:

> I'm sure you'll be happy to know I just got fucked and didn't have time to come.

Jon:

> That's not very nice of them.

The winking emoji he adds tells me he doesn't mean what he's saying.

Miranda:

> I know it's not. Now I have a pussy full of Mr. Jacobs' cum. How am I supposed to work in these conditions?

His reply makes my body buzz with delight.

Jon:

> Send me a picture of that used pussy.

Well, that's hot. I rush to the bathroom and pull my skirt and panties back down before bending over the sink. It takes a couple of tries with the camera behind me, before I get a picture that shows the perfect angle where he can see my swollen, wet pussy.

I send it to him and his reply comes right as I get back to my desk.

Jon:

> Beautiful. I'm heading into a meeting. Have fun today, Kitten.

I stare at the wall in a daze. What is my life? I'm a mess. I don't know what's planned and what isn't—is it even a real meeting? It's only 10 a.m. and something tells me it's going to be a long day of sexual torture. I'm 100 percent on board with this plan.

Chapter 2

I attempt to work for the next hour, but all I can do is think about being fucked again. Will one of the other lawyers fuck me too, or is today only for Mr. Jacobs? He's no spring chicken, so how many times can he come in a day? He might need a break.

The meeting must be over now, because the hallway fills with sound a moment before the whole group passes my desk on the way out, and I blush, focusing on my computer screen to avoid looking at any of them. Shit, I hope the room didn't smell like sex. I wasn't exactly paying attention when I left.

Once the other lawyers are out of earshot, Mr. Jacobs saunters up to my desk, carrying a bundle of files. "Go clean up the conference room. When you're done, copy all these reports before lunch."

He sets them on my desk and I eye the stack. Oh, I've been here before. ..I'll clean and then as I'm making copies, someone is going to come in and fuck me against the copier. Just watch.

As he walks off, he adds over his shoulder. "If you get it done by lunch, I'll spank you. If not..."

Well hell, I'm about to be the fastest copy girl ever.

"Yes, sir," I call out sweetly and hurry to clean.

As soon as I step inside the conference room, I'm met with the faint aroma of musk in the air. It smells like me—did all the lawyers notice? I'm suddenly dying of embarrassment. I'm sure they didn't, and I only do because I know what sex with me smells like...right? Right.

The pile of folders I stuffed is at the end of the table and catches my eye. None of them have been touched. Yeah, Mr. Jacobs gave me a stupid task just so he could fuck me. I bet he never planned to let me come.

I'm grumbling to myself as I give the room a cursory cleaning. I can't spend too long in here since I actually want that spanking—and the potential fucking while I make those copies. I grab the files from my desk and dash to the copier machine. I keep one eye on the doorway while I run the files through the machine. Who is going to come in? Maybe Mr. Parks, since he most likely knows what happened in the conference room. I'm on the edge the entire time, just waiting.

No one shows up.

Before I leave the copier room, I check the wall clock. Twenty minutes to spare. Someone could have fucked me, and I still would have gotten done in time. These guys are wasting their opportunities.

I huff and take the copies back to my desk. Before I can sit down, Mr. Jacobs appears. "Bring those with you."

Excitement surges in my veins as I grab the papers and follow him to his office. He steps aside at the doorway and gestures for me to enter his lair. As I pass him, his hand lightly connects with my ass. There'll probably be more of that shortly. I'm not sure I've ever been this eager for a spanking—but then again, have I ever waited two whole years for someone to spank me?

"Put the copies on my desk and then strip." The raw edge in his tone makes me tremble with desire.

Oooh, here we go. He moves behind his desk as I toss the files onto the surface, scattering them haphazardly. I watch with satisfaction as some of the papers slide out.

"Oops, sorry." I try to sound apologetic as I turn around and show him my backside. I'm just ensuring I get a good spanking.

I unzip my skirt ever so slowly and let it fall to the floor as I start to unbutton my shirt. Mr. Jacobs sighs as if I'm exasperating him and says, "Face me."

I spin around and spread my shirt open so he can see my white lace bra. Teasing him is so much fun, and I love riling him up. It will make him all that much rougher when he finally spanks me good.

"Sexy," he says under his breath, his face warming as his eyes feast on my breasts.

That's when it dawns on me. I keep moaning about how Bonny made it so I couldn't fuck my bosses for two years, but it's the same from his side of the fence. It's been a very long time since we've played these games, and he's probably just as wound up as I am. The knowledge sends a ripple of pleasure through me, and I feel like a powerful, sexual goddess.

As soon as I toss my shirt on the floor, he demands, "Come here and put your elbows on my desk."

Oooh, someone is impatient. He didn't even let me undress all the way. I sway my hips as I brush past him and assume the requested position, placing my elbows and palms against the scattered paperwork. I wiggle my backside at him, feeling the stretch of satin and lace across my butt. He caresses my inner thigh before sliding his hand upwards. I rest my forehead on the backs of my hands as a tingling sensation zips straight to my pussy. It's crazy how he only has to touch me and I'm ready to beg him to fuck me.

He hooks a finger into the edge of my panties and pulls it up between the cheeks of my ass. The fabric bunches together and digs into my pussy. Mmm, fuck. I jiggle my ass again, trying to make the fabric rub my clit, but it doesn't move.

He slides a finger into my pussy. "Tell me about Jon."

Jon? Why is he asking about my husband while his finger is inside me?

Before I can ask him why the heck he's bringing this up, he adds another finger. My brain blanks. Uh...what were we talking about? I push my hips back, forcing his fingers in deeper.

He slaps my ass with his free hand, and I wobble in my heels for a moment as heat rushes through me.

"Answer my question."

The spank clears my head and I remember the topic. "Things are going great with Jon."

I'm still not sure why he's asking, and my brain is quickly short-circuiting. Being spanked earlier got me hot and bothered, and I'm still tender from his little show in the conference room.

"How many other guys have you fucked in the last two years?"

I tense, suddenly apprehensive. Where's he going with this?

"Miranda," he growls.

"I don't know," I respond softly. It's weird discussing this with Mr. Jacobs. "The freeuse resort you sent me to had at least a dozen men."

Shit, did all the guys fuck me at the resort? Even though it was only a few weeks ago, my memory of that weekend is a bit hazy. I was so blissed out, I mostly remember the room full of naked guys in Santa hats as they took turns using my mouth.

I rock my hips up and down, trying to force him to finger fuck me harder.

Instead he pulls his hand away. "Naughty slut," he says a moment before his hand connects with my ass.

A pleasurable pain blossoms across my backside and I moan softly. That was a firm hit, and it drives home the fact that he's in charge. My pulse speeds up as I wait to see if he's going to spank me, finger me, or fuck me.

He presses his hand against my pussy, applying pressure but this time he doesn't slide his fingers inside. "You're hoping I fuck you again, aren't you?"

Um...of course I am. I'm not crazy.

I give a breathy, "Please, I want your cock. I'll be a good girl for the rest of the day."

The devil knows that's a promise I'll break at the next available opportunity. But if it gets me fucked or spanked right this moment, I can pretend I'll be good.

He chuckles. "It's a shame you don't deserve it."

I snap my head up and look back at him. Um, what?

My mind spins in confusion as he says, "But I could be convinced and change my mind. Why do you deserve an orgasm?"

He's not supposed to make me justify my desires. He's supposed to just use me! He spanks me again, and I whimper. "I made the folders, set up the coffee, and cleaned."

"Not enough." Another sharp smack.

Shit, what else did I do? I wrack my brain, trying to think of anything else I've done that might warrant a reward. "I...I made copies. I did everything you asked."

"You're missing the point, Miranda."

A painful spank makes me groan as he continues to swat me, alternating cheeks. Each time he makes contact, my ass flares with heat. Within moments, my pussy is practically dripping. I enjoy Mr. Jacobs being grumpy and making me jump through hoops to get what I want...as long as I get what I want eventually.

After a series of powerful strikes, he asks again, "Tell me. What have you done today that deserves an orgasm?"

The correct answer is probably "nothing," since I apparently haven't done enough, but the overwhelming need to be fucked makes me beg. "I'll do anything you want," I babble. "Please..."

Pain explodes across my backside as his hand makes contact again. Ouch. Fuck. Oww. I rest my head on the surface of his desk and close my eyes. Jon never spanks me like this, and something inside me loosens. A warm fuzziness steals over me and I rise above the pain to where all I can feel is pleasure. My awareness narrows to just the satisfying jolts and the slickness between my thighs

I'm shocked when I climax. One second I'm in a peaceful place, and the next moment I'm flying high as an orgasm rockets through me. I cry out as my entire body spasms. Oooh no.

He stops spanking me. "Did you have permission to come?"

I mean, I didn't not have permission. He never said I couldn't. I don't voice my thought. "I'm sorry, sir. I couldn't stop it."

He massages the sore globes of my bottom for a few moments before moving up to unhook my bra. His warm palms caressing my breasts are wonderful, and I relax as he fondles me. At this moment, he really could do whatever he wanted and I'd love it.

CHAPTER 3

I expect Mr. Jacobs to fuck me now that he's spanked me, but he sits in his chair and gives my butt a gentle pat. "Ready to work again?"

Ugh, work. When I try to stand up, he presses his hand on my back. "Stay there. This position is perfect."

A zip of desire runs through me and I relax. I'm up for whatever involves being bent over his desk.

A knock on the door makes me jump, and Mr. Jacobs calls out, "Come in."

Mr. Parks and Mr. Daniels walk in, and take seats across from us. They smile at me as Mr. Jacobs hands me a legal pad and pen. "Take the minutes for our meeting. You'll type them up after."

What kind of meeting are they having with an almost naked woman in front of them? I wiggle my ass to tease Mr. Jacobs. My panties are still wedged together and driving me crazy.

"The clients are demanding..." Mr. Jacobs starts.

Mr. Parks snorts. "They always are."

I'm going to be demanding if I don't get fucked soon. My handwriting is a mess as I try to force myself to follow their boring conversation about a local conference Mr. Daniels is attending tomorrow. When Mr. Jacobs starts fingering my clit, I bite my lip to hold in a moan. I should have expected this.

Mr. Jacobs keeps talking like nothing's happening while he slides his fingers into my pussy and fucks me with them. I struggle to write, my hand shaking from pleasure. It doesn't help that Mr. Daniels and Mr. Parks are watching me. I can tell they're amused.

A jolt of electricity shoots through me as he speeds up his hand movements. My brain goes fuzzy as I barrel towards another orgasm. I can barely manage to write anything. What were they saying?

I'm distracted by the bulges in Mr. Parks' and Mr. Daniels' pants. My mouth waters, imagining sucking them both. Why aren't they all using me if I'm their freeuse toy this week? Or are they taking turns like they used to?

"Miranda." Mr. Jacobs pulls his fingers out and smacks my butt. "Be a good office slut. Crawl over there and take care of them. Your moans are distracting."

Oops, I didn't realize I was moaning. Is he suggesting what I think? I glance over my shoulder at him, questioningly. He gives a slight nod towards the other lawyers. Fuck yes, he wants me to suck their cocks.

I kick off my heels and sink to my knees. Mr. Parks spreads his legs as I crawl over, a thrill shooting through me at the power I wield. My fingers fumble with his belt buckle because I'm so damn eager to get him into my mouth. When I finally free his cock, I pause to appreciate it. He's rock-hard and ready.

I trace my fingertips along his length, savoring the silky texture. God, I love giving blow jobs. A glistening bead forms at the tip, and my mouth waters. I wrap my lips around him, rolling my tongue over the head. He fills my mouth perfectly, and I relish his every twitch and groan. Knowing I'm the source of his pleasure gives me satisfaction. I take him deeper, my own arousal building with each inch.

"Fuck, that's good," he groans, his fingers tangling in my hair.

I hum around him, the vibration making him buck his hips. His reaction spurs me on, and I hollow my cheeks, sucking harder. The taste of him floods my senses, salty and masculine. I press my thighs together, seeking relief. My panties are still bunched up, but they're firmly lodged in a way that only makes me aware of them and doesn't give me enough pleasure.

"Let's finish our meeting," Mr. Jacobs says casually.

They return to their business discussion while I bob my head. I'm getting wetter by the second.

"Miranda, pay attention. You'll still need to write this down," Mr. Jacobs reminds me, with a hint of amusement.

Yeah, these notes I write up later aren't going to be thorough. I'll just have to make them all come so they're happy and don't care. When Mr. Jacobs mentions me going to the conference with Mr. Daniels tomorrow, I perk up. A field trip! Wait...is Mr. Daniels going to fuck me there?

I keep sucking Mr. Parks while daydreaming about being passed around by a dozen horny lawyers. The fantasy makes me quicken my pace, desperate to taste his cum.

"Fuck, I'm close," Mr. Parks hisses.

I double my efforts, my hand working what my mouth can't reach. His hips flex, and I know he's right there. With a final groan, he explodes, flooding my mouth. I swallow greedily, not wanting to waste a drop.

As his grip on my hair loosens, I give him one last lick and pull back with a smile. "Mmm...tasty."

I'm dying for a cock to fuck me—anyone's cock—but Mr. Daniels is staring at me hungrily. Without being told, I crawl between his legs.

Mr. Jacobs sighs. "Suck him off. Make it quick."

That's not quite what I had in mind, but oh well. Mr. Daniels pulls out his thick cock for me, and I eagerly take him into my mouth, savoring his salty taste and the difference between the two men's cocks. He moans when I take him deep, his tip hitting the back of my throat. I cup his balls as I bob faster, determined to make him come quickly. It doesn't take long before his thigh muscles tense and he blows his load. I clean him up with my tongue before sitting back. That was a job well done, if I do say so myself.

The men look well satisfied—well, not Mr. Jacobs. And where is Mr. King today? Why wasn't he at the meeting? I wait for instructions as Mr. Daniels and Mr. Parks straighten their clothes and leave. I guess the meeting is over.

"Think you can write a coherent report?" Mr. Jacobs asks.

I stay silent. Uhh, doubtful. But I can wing it. He beckons me over and I crawl to him, hoping he'll let me suck his dick next. To my surprise, he pulls out a packet of trail mix from his desk drawer and feeds it to me while I kneel on the floor next to him.

Between bites, I ask, "What's this about the conference, sir?"

My pussy throbs, craving his cock. I need to come so badly. Hopefully once he stops feeding me, he'll fuck me.

"We thought our freeuse toy might like an outing," he says. "Have some fun outside the office."

Uh... "Fun with other lawyers?" If this is some gangbang, I need to talk to Jon.

Mr. Jacobs laughs. "No, just Mr. Daniels. You'll have to be discreet. Think you can manage that?"

"I'll be the most discreet slut ever," I promise.

"We're counting on it." He touches my cheek gently, making my stomach flutter. Then his voice turns stern. "Now go type those notes. Email them to me and be back here in fifteen minutes."

"Yes, sir." The air crackles between us—we both know what's coming when I return.

"Leave your clothes. You'll get them when the report's done."

Oooh, fuck. My heart races as I murmur, "Yes, sir."

He nods, satisfied. "Good. Now get to work."

I walk to my desk, hyperaware I'm only wearing my panties. What if a client shows up? My nipples harden from the thrill of possible exposure.

My pussy is drenched and I eye my office chair. Do men even think of these problems? Just go type these up, he says...how am I supposed to sit on my chair like this?

Fuck. I sneak to the break room and grab a cardigan I brought in last week and forgot on the coat rack, tying it around my waist as a makeshift skirt. Not perfect, but it'll do. I rush back, my heart pounding with nervous excitement. The risk of getting caught sends shivers down my spine.

I sit down, glad for the extra padding against my sore ass, and start typing. I try to remember the meeting details through my sex-fogged brain, but the taste of cum in my mouth and the wetness between my legs cloud my thoughts.

I'm almost done when footsteps approach. Shit. Shit. Shit. My heart leaps as Mr. King walks up.

"Miranda, are the notes ready? Mr. Jacobs told me to ask you for a copy," he says casually, though his gaze lingers on my body.

I swallow hard. "Almost. I can email them to you shortly."

He nods, his eyes dropping to my breasts. "You're making me wish it was my turn with you again."

Ooh, so they ARE taking turns. My body vibrates with delight at the thought.

Once he leaves, I quickly finish and email Mr. Jacobs and Mr. King. I'm sure it's missing details, but it's the best I could do under the circumstances. I rush back to Mr. Jacobs' office, leaving the cardigan behind. That thing needs a good wash now.

I knock softly before entering. He looks up, his expression hardened. "Those notes were unacceptable. You missed half the conversation."

No shit. I clasp my hands, purposely making my breasts squish together. "I'm sorry, sir. I was distracted."

By his fingers in my pussy before I sucked on two cocks.

"Come here."

His expression is unreadable and he stands as I come around to his side. He slides my panties down my legs and I step out of them. When he lifts me onto his desk, I wince as the hard wood presses against my tender backside.

He grins and spreads my knees. Yeah, he knows my ass hurts. He kisses my neck. "Did you think if you looked sexy that I wouldn't notice how bad of a job you did?"

I shiver, my body responding to him. "I'm sorry, sir. I can try again—"

"Try again?" His look turns predatory. "Or maybe I'll just fuck you to remind you who's in charge."

Yep, I like his plan better. He pushes me back onto the desk so that I'm lying down and tugs me to the edge. His fingers probe my pussy, making him growl, "You're so fucking wet."

I squirm, aching for more. "Please fuck me, sir."

He pulls out his cock, stroking it slowly. "You need this?"

"Yes, please." I nod eagerly and wrap my legs around him.

He taps the head against my clit. "Beg for it."

I gyrate my hips and whimper, "Please, sir. Please fuck me. I need your cock inside me. I'll do better next time. Please just fuck me."

He grasps my waist with both hands and thrusts in hard. "Ooooh, god," I cry out and arch my back as he starts fucking me fast and rough. I throw my hands over my head so I can hold on to the desk's edge as he ravages me. The sound of skin slapping fills the room as I get closer to my climax.

"You're such a good little slut. You love being fucked like this, don't you?"

I gasp, "Yes, so good," as the pressure builds with each stroke. I'm ready to explode.

He reaches between my legs to rub my clit. "Show me how much you love being our office slut and come for me."

The combined stimulation is too much. Ecstasy rips through me, and I come so hard I see stars. I convulse around his cock as he fucks me through my orgasm.

He doesn't slow down. "You're going to come once more before I fill you up and send you home to your husband."

The desk creaks as he hammers into me and continues to rub my clit. Another orgasm builds as I think about going home to Jon full of Mr. Jacobs' cum. My husband is going to love hearing about my day.

Mr. Jacobs is relentless, and time loses meaning. I play with my nipples, and chant, "Oh my god," as delight twists in my core. He's hitting the good spot deep inside me repeatedly, and I'm ready to come.

His thrusts become shorter, and I finally snap. I scream as another orgasm tears through me. He pulls out slowly without coming, and I feel a rush of wetness leaking out. I hope he has some of those wet wipes in here.

"Look at you, all fucked and messy," he says, appreciatively. "You want more, don't you? You want me to fuck you like the slut you are?"

"Yes, please."

He grabs my arms and pulls me up from the desk. His eyes are heavy with lust, mirroring the hunger in my own. He lifts me off my feet, and I hook my legs around his waist, crossing my ankles behind his back.

His hands grip my butt, fingers digging into the tender flesh as he holds me up. I can feel his hard cock pressing against my entrance, and I'm desperate for him to fill me again.

"Where should I fuck you next?"

He sounds like he's talking to himself, but I answer anyway. "Everywhere."

He carries me over to the couch that was recently added to his office, laying me down on my back. He slowly takes his clothes off and I watch him, curious to see if he looks different than I remember. He's still fit and trim, and I can tell he still exercises regularly.

Once he's naked, he looks down at me and commands, "Spread your legs for me."

I obey, letting him see how swollen and wet my pussy is. He kneels between my legs and moves his face to my pussy. I can feel his breath on my sensitive flesh, and I shiver with anticipation.

"You're absolutely gorgeous like this," he groans. He leans in and licks a slow path up my pussy, my hips rocking as he teases me.

"God, you're delicious." He dips his tongue inside me, and I reach down to grip his hair as he feasts on me.

He pulls back, holding my gaze. "You want my cock, don't you? You want me to fuck you until you can't think straight?"

I'm so turned on, all I can do is say, "Yes."

In reality, he can do whatever he wants. I'm beyond caring. He could stop right now, and I'd probably just thank him for using me.

He grabs my legs, pushing my knees towards my chest and I can feel myself opening up for him.

He slams into me, his hips pistoning as he fucks me hard and fast. I can feel every inch of him, every ridge and vein as he slides in and out of me.

He leans forward, holding onto my thighs as he uses them for leverage. His thrusts become harder and I continuously moan in pleasure.

"You feel so good." His muscles strain as he pounds into me.

I take back everything I thought earlier about him being the oldest. This guy is a machine. He has me pinned to the couch and at his mercy. It's amazing.

"You're just our little toy, a plaything to use whenever we need a release," he groans, and my body lights up at his words.

I gasp when he hits a pleasurable spot repeatedly, and my head spins. He teased me for hours, but this was worth the wait.

"You like that, don't you?" he asks. "Knowing we're going to use you all the time." The raw need in his husky voice sends another tremor of pleasure along my spine.

"Yes, I'm your fucktoy to use. Want it!"

I'd say anything, do anything, I just need to come again, and I need him to fill me up. I can tell the next orgasm is going to be massive. My body is on fire, every nerve ending alive as the tension coils tighter and tighter.

I'm ready to fall, and I moan, "Feels so good."

His tone is harsh as he hammers into me. "Come for me, you little slut. Come for me NOW."

"Fuck!" I scream, as my body shudders. The pleasure is so intense I see flashes of light behind my eyelids as I ride the waves of rapture. It might have lasted a few seconds, or a minute, I'm so far gone it feels like it's never ending.

With a final, deep thrust, he finds his own release. It seems like he's fucking me forever, unloading ropes and ropes of cum inside me, filling me up.

I'm shivering when he collapses on top of me. We're a tangle of limbs and sweat, our breathing ragged and uneven. I can feel him still inside me, his cock slowly softening as we both come down from the high.

I'm not sure how long we lie there, blissed out. But eventually his lips brush against my ear.

"You're amazing," he whispers.

A warmth spreads through me as he helps me sit up. When he kisses me, I'm not expecting it. It's a gentle kiss, but thorough, and as our tongues twirl together, I realize this is something I'm going to have to tell Jon about. Mr. Jacobs has changed over the last two years. There's an unexpected softness to him, but I think I'm going to enjoy it. He can still spank me and fuck me hard, and I know Jon is fine with my play partners being tender towards me.

Mr. Jacobs breaks off the kiss, and murmurs, "Good girl. Now I'm sending you home early because you need a good night's sleep for the conference tomorrow."

Ooh, yeah, the conference. I'm still tingling from my orgasms and give him a saucy smile. "Yes, sir. Thank you, sir."

He laughs and helps me stand up. "Now clean up and go home."

When he hands me my clothes, my body aches pleasantly as I slowly dress. As I leave his office, I make sure to sway my hips so he gets a nice view...and I want him thinking about spanking me again sometime soon.

CHAPTER 4

I call Jon on my drive home, putting him on speaker.

"Hey, Kitten. How was your day?"

The sound of his voice instantly turns me on again, and my body hums with lust. "Eventful. I've got stories to tell."

He laughs. "I'm sure you do, and I can't wait to hear them. Bad news though, I'm stuck here. I might be late."

My excitement deflates. "Nooo, you need to be home soon."

"I know, I'm sorry. I'll make it up to you later, promise."

I sigh and grumble, "Fine. Guess I'll have to entertain myself. Blame work if I'm too exhausted when you get home."

He teases, "Start without me, but you aren't allowed to finish until I get there."

Shit. Heat pools between my thighs. "Hurry home."

"Will do, Kitten. Love you."

"Love you too," I say, hanging up as I pull into our driveway.

As soon as I'm inside the house, I head for the bedroom, removing my clothes as I go. I don't bother putting anything on. I lie back on the bed, letting my mind wander over the day's events—the spankings, the thrill of fucking Mr. Jacobs again. I slide my hand down to my clit, teasing myself, but it's not enough. I grab my phone and text Jon.

Miranda:

You leaving yet?

He responds instantly.

Jon:

Yes, fuck work. I'm walking out the door right now. Keep that pussy warm for me.

Oooh, nice. His office is only 15 minutes away. I play with myself, moving my hand slowly so I don't accidentally come.

I hear the garage door open and then Jon is in the room, looking as eager as I feel.

"Hey, Kitten," he says in that husky tone of his that tells me he's half crazed already.

I spread my legs wider and he eyes my pussy as he strips. I bet he's trying to see some of my boss's cum.

Once he's naked, he crawls onto the bed next to me and kisses me deeply. I taste his urgency, his need. I love how much he gets turned on by me fucking other people.

Between kisses, he growls, "Tell me everything."

He slips his hand between my legs, and I arch against him as he rubs my clit. How am I supposed to think, let alone talk, while he's touching me? But this is the game we play, and I'm going to tell him everything because that's what keeps our relationship strong.

As he trails kisses down my neck, across my collarbone, and to my breast, I tell him about my day. "I was bent over the desk, and they had a meeting while Mr. Jacobs fingered me."

"Mmm, nice," he moans and takes a nipple into his mouth. He sucks hard and pleasure shoots straight to my core.

While I tell him about the conference and sucking on the lawyers during the meeting, he continues to tease me, circling my clit, dipping his fingers inside me and making me squirm.

I rock against him. "Jon...please."

His eyes smolder with need. "Please what, Kitten?"

"Fuck me," I beg. "Need you inside me."

He grins and positions himself, fitting his cock against my pussy. He doesn't make me wait, and he presses in slowly—oh god, I wish he would pound into me. I love it when he fucks me slow, and yet I also hate it.

As he thrusts into me at his own pace, his cock hits all the right places. I wrap my legs around him and hold onto his shoulders, pulling him closer. Our moans fill the room. I'm close, so close.

I whimper, "Oh, god. I'm almost there."

He looks at me with a fierce expression. "Thank me for letting you fuck your bosses."

"Thank you," I gasp out, my body trembling with the effort to hold back my orgasm. "Thank you for letting me be their fucktoy."

He speeds up slightly, his thrusts hitting me deeper. "That's right, Kitten. You're my little slut, and I love sharing you."

His words send me spiraling and I mewl out in pleasure.

"Good girl," he murmurs. "Now come for me."

I cry out and let go, writhing as the pleasure explodes through me.

My orgasm triggers his. "Fuck, Miranda," he gasps, his cock pulsing inside me, filling me with cum.

We rock together as he finishes unloading, and when he rolls off me, he pulls me close. I'm a puddle of joy as I lay my head on his chest, listening to his heartbeat slow.

"So, tell me more about tomorrow," he says, his voice rumbling under my ear.

I smile, tracing hearts on his chest. "I'll be going with Mr. Daniels. Mr. Jacobs said we'll need to be discreet."

"I'm sure you can handle that," he chuckles. "I want you to have fun, so be their good little slut."

"I will," I purr, snuggling closer.

He kisses the top of my head. "And call me when you get home tomorrow. I want to hear all about it."

"Always, my love."

As we lie there, basking in the afterglow, a sense of contentment washes over me. This is what I love about our relationship. The openness, the trust, the shared pleasure. I'm truly living my best life as a hotwife. And I'm looking forward to whatever happens at the conference. I'm ready to be a slut again for Mr. Daniels.

The End

FREEUSE OFFICE HOURS

SHARED WITH THE BOSS

LACEY CROSS

CHAPTER 1

Mr. Daniels' black sedan idles in my driveway at 7:30 sharp. I've been turned on since the moment I woke up, and I have high hopes for our day out of the office. After yesterday's office shenanigans with Mr. Jacobs, I'm eager to see how the most reserved lawyer at the firm handles having a personal freeuse slut for the day.

He's looking mighty fine this morning. His broad shoulders fill out his light blue dress shirt, which contrasts nicely against his rich brown skin. I pause for a moment to adjust my long brown hair, secured in a single braid, before admiring the view and opening the passenger door.

"Good morning." His deep voice wraps around me as I slide into the seat. His gaze travels down my body, lingering on the flared black skirt and lavender blouse Jon picked out. "You look lovely today."

Heat pools between my legs at his appreciative tone. Mmm, I've always loved his voice, especially when he's turned on. Being the firm's designated entertainment this week is turning out better than I'd hoped. I imagine him bending me over a desk, hiking up this same skirt.

"Thank you, sir." The word 'sir' rolls off my tongue with a delicious little thrill. I've grown to enjoy calling him that, each time sending a subtle shiver down my spine. I cross my legs, inching my skirt up to reveal a glimpse of bare thigh above my stockings. His eyes dart to the exposed skin before snapping back to the road.

The sexual tension thickens the air as we hit the highway. I study his profile, wondering if I'll need to drop hints or flat-out beg him to fuck me today. For a man built like a walking wet dream, he keeps his desires locked down tight, even after Mr. Jacobs arranged this special week where I'm available for all their pleasure.

"Looking forward to the conference?" I ask, probing his mood. This conference agenda isn't exactly thrilling, but being alone with Mr. Daniels away from the office certainly is. The corner of his mouth lifts in a half-smile that makes my core clench.

"It could be fun." His deep voice warms with a hint of playfulness. "That convention center does have a lot of...private spaces."

Oh thank fuck. Maybe I won't have to work too hard to seduce him after all.

A shiver runs through me as his large hand settles on my thigh, his thumb tracing circles on the sensitive skin above my stocking. Each stroke sends sparks straight to my pussy.

"Is that so?" I part my legs slightly, giving him better access. Between keynote speakers and networking events, there'll be breaks where he can use me however he wants.

His fingers creep higher under my skirt. "I think we'll find plenty of opportunities to make the day productive."

My breath hitches as his hand slides further up. It looks like Mr. Daniels might have some delicious plans for me today. I'm starting to think Mr. Jacobs knew exactly what he was doing when he assigned me to accompany our most reserved partner to this conference.

The convention center is attached to a hotel, and he parks in the garage in a secluded corner. Once the car is off, he turns to me. "Ready?"

I grab my oversized purse and flash him my most innocent smile. "Always ready, sir."

The registration desk feels miles away, and as we walk, each brush of his arm against mine sets my skin on fire. He checks us in for the conference, and I barely listen. I'm daydreaming of all the places he could fuck me at the hotel. Where can people find private places in a very public setting when it doesn't include spending the night?

We navigate through the crowd of suits and pencil skirts toward the keynote room. His hand hovers at my lower back, not quite touching but close enough that I feel his heat seeping into my skin.

"Let's sit in the back." He gestures to empty seats.

I nod and slide past him, knowing he's watching every sway of my hips. Our legs brush as we settle in and the lights dim. Some CEO takes the stage and drones about AI and legal tech. Mr. Daniels' "accidental" touches to my knee make it impossible to think. The scent of his cologne envelops me, and all I can think about are those private spaces he mentioned.

"Interesting stuff," he whispers against my ear. His hand inches higher on my thigh, and I bite back a moan.

I shift in my seat, desperate for friction. His fingers tighten on my leg when I cross and uncross my legs, but he keeps watching the speaker like he isn't driving me wild.

I glance around the conference room, making sure the other attendees are absorbed in the presentation. Perfect—no one's looking this way. Time to play dirty.

I adjust my position, letting my skirt ride up higher. His hand freezes, and even though he doesn't move it up any further, the weight of his hand is driving me crazy.

The CEO rambles about algorithms while I conduct my own experiment in breaking Mr. Daniels' control. I spread my leg slowly so his hand grazes my inner thigh. His fingers flex, and I can tell he wants to move them to my pussy.

"Pay attention," he murmurs. "You'll need to brief the partners on this presentation."

"I am, sir. I'm a *very* good multitasker."

To show him what I mean, I slide my hand onto his leg. When his jaw clenches, a thrill ripples through me. Oh yeah, he's getting worked up. My panties are soaked, and we haven't even found those quiet corners yet.

God, I hope he fucks me before lunch.

CHAPTER 2

"Fifteen minutes until the next session," Mr. Daniels says, his voice low as we exit the keynote. His hand finds my back, more assertive than ever. "Follow me."

He guides me through the crowds, down a side corridor, and into the parking garage. Each step amplifies the pulsing beat of my heart.

He pins me against his car, hands planted firmly on either side of my shoulders. "These past couple of years," he murmurs, his dark eyes burning into mine, "I've had a lot of time to think about how I used to fuck you at the office. But we've both changed."

The heat of him and the woodsy scent of his cologne is making it difficult to think. "And how have you changed?" I manage to ask.

"I'm not hesitant anymore." His lips curl into a confident smile as he trails one finger down my neck, following the line of my blouse to the swell of my cleavage. "I like to go for what I want now."

Christ, this new side of him—commanding, sure of himself—practically has me panting. His massive hands slide down to grip my hips, and I arch into his touch.

"Ask me what I want," he demands.

Oooh, I like where this is going. "What exactly do you want, sir?"

"I want to show you how much I appreciate all you taught me. I've been putting it to good use since then."

Wait, what did I teach him? I don't have time to ask before he captures my mouth in a searing kiss that makes my knees weak. His tongue sweeps inside, claiming me thoroughly while his hands roam over my body. When he pulls back, we're both breathing hard.

"Turn around, slut," he orders. "Hands on the car.

I comply instantly, pressing my palms against the cool metal. Mmm, I'll be his slut. I definitely like this new dominant tone.

He kicks my feet apart, then runs his hands up my thighs, pushing my skirt to my waist. I'm trembling, and it's a toss-up on whether it's the cool air in the garage or my need for his cock that's doing it.

His fingers tease the edge of my stockings. "Such a good girl. Wearing these to please me." He slides his hand to my panties and presses against the damp spot. "Already so wet for me."

I whimper as he rubs me through the silk. He's right, and I did wear the stockings for him. Jon picked out my outfit and he liked the idea of me looking respectable to everyone else, but a sex kitten underneath my clothes.

Mr. Daniels increases the pressure of his fingers, and I rock against him, desperate to get something inside me. Since he parked in a secluded corner, we're far from the traffic flow. Almost like this was planned—smart man—but my eyes catch a glint of something dark mounted on a nearby pillar. Is that a security camera? The thought of being recorded, of some-one watching this later, gives me a naughty zing.

"Remember what you are?" He hooks his fingers on the waistband of my panties and pauses. "You're our freeuse toy this week. *My* toy right now."

"Yes, sir," I gasp. When he tugs my panties down, I'm dizzy with need. When is the last time I was fucked in a parking lot? It's been a long time.

"You taught me how to take what I want." His fingers trace the seam of my pussy, and I shimmy my hips, trying to entice him to slide his fingers inside me as he continues. "You made me realize how much I enjoy watching you submit."

Holy shit. This is a man on a mission to wreck me.

He removes his hand from my pussy long enough to get his cock out. I feel the thick head of it press against me, and I bite my lip to stifle a moan.

"Such a greedy little slut," he growls. "Letting me fuck you where anyone could see us."

Ohhh, god. He sinks his cock into me, and my head whirls from pleasure. He doesn't take his time with it—not that we have much time— and his thrusts are deep and steady. I keep my hands flat on the car to steady myself as he sets a relentless pace.

"Stay quiet," he warns, one hand on my hip, the other tugging on my long braid. "Unless you want the whole parking garage to hear you."

The danger of being caught makes my heart race faster. Every footstep, every distant voice, amplifies the thrill. But all I can focus on is his cock driving into me.

"That's it," he grunts, pulling my hair tighter, forcing my head back. "Take it like the good little freeuse fucktoy you are."

Jesus, was he taking notes all this time? I love his dirty talk. My orgasm builds quickly, pressure tightening in my core.

"Sir, please," I whimper, not sure if I'm going to have time to come. His thrusts grow harder, deeper, making the car rock, and I have the insane urge to laugh when I hear the beep of his key fob, like he's just turned the car alarm off before we set it off.

He can tell I'm distracted; he whacks against my pussy hard, making me gasp as the pleasure skyrockets through me.

"Come for me," he orders. "Come for me before I blow my load and you have to wait until lunch time. Unless you want to feel my cum dripping out of you while you're desperate and horny."

Oh nooo! The thought of being unfilled is what tips me over the edge. Pleasure crashes over me, and I muffle my scream against my arm.

He follows right after, grinding deep as he fills me. He jerks against me a few times, unloading ropes of sticky cum before he stills. For a moment, we just breathe together, his chest pressed against my back.

"Next session starts in five minutes," he says, his voice returning to its usual professional tone as he helps me straighten up. But there's a new spark in his eyes when I turn to him. "Better fix your hair. You look thoroughly fucked."

My mind is fried, and I can't wait to see what else he has planned.

My legs are still shaking as we slip into our seats for the morning breakout session. He was right, and I can feel his cum leaking into my panties. I squirm, and it earns me a knowing smirk from Mr. Daniels.

"Problem?" he whispers, sitting there cool as a cucumber, like he didn't just fuck me senseless in the parking garage.

I just lift my eyebrow at him and try to focus on the presentation about legal document automation. After a few minutes, his hand finds my thigh under the table. His thumb traces lazy circles on my stockings, each touch sending aftershocks straight to my core. My skin is so sensitive I might come just from him stroking it.

I need to tell Jon about this new, commanding version of Mr. Daniels. Carefully angling my phone away from prying eyes, I type to my husband.

Miranda:

> Holy shit babe. Mr. Daniels just fucked me against his car in the parking garage. When did he get so dominant?

Jon's reply is almost instant.

Jon:

That's my good little slut. Is he taking care of you properly?

Miranda:

Fuck yes. Still leaking his cum during this presentation about...something. Can't focus.

"Miranda." Mr. Daniels' voice is quiet but firm. "Pay attention."

I bite my lip, hyper-aware of his massive hand still resting on my thigh. Jon's next text makes me stifle a giggle because it matches what Mr. Daniels said.

Jon:

Better focus kitten, or he might have to punish you later

The thought of Mr. Daniels punishing me makes my pussy clench. There's no way he would have previously done it, but this new version of him? It's possible. His fingers tighten slightly on my leg, like he knows exactly what I'm thinking about.

The presenter drones on about workflow optimization, but all I can do is think about Mr. Daniels and his wandering hand. Every few minutes, he moves closer to my pussy, testing my ability to maintain my composure.

Fuckity, fuck, fuck, fuck. His middle finger traces the lace of my stockings, and I have to fake a cough to cover my moan.

"Shhh," he murmurs, eyes still fixed on the presenter. "Unless you want everyone to know what a desperate little slut you are?"

Yep, it's official. He's trying to kill me with his teasing.

"Twenty minutes until lunch," Mr. Daniels whispers close to my ear, his fingertips now dancing along my inner thigh. "I already know exactly what I'm going to do to you."

Christ. I press my thighs together, earning a warning squeeze from his hand.

This is going to be the longest conference of my life.

CHAPTER 3

The lunch break can't come fast enough. Once we're free, Mr. Daniels practically drags me away from the networking crowd, his fingers locked around my wrist.

"In here." He opens a supply closet door, checking both ways before pulling me inside. The lock clicks shut, and suddenly, I'm pinned against the wall, his massive body caging me in.

"Sir—" I start, but he silences me with a fierce kiss.

"Shh." His voice is pure grit. "You've been taunting me all morning with those little squirms and sighs."

My pulse quickens, and his hands slide up my thighs, bunching my skirt. The closet is cramped, smelling of paper and cleaning supplies, but who cares? His fingers find my drenched panties. "Still wet from earlier?" he growls against my neck. "You filthy girl."

Damn, if I had known he'd turned into a dirty talker, I would have been even more unhappy when not fucking my bosses at work the last couple of years. I press my back against the wall as he tugs my underwear down.

"Step out of them," he commands, and I slip off my heels so they don't get caught in them as I do what he wants.

"Now, open that pretty mouth."

Uh, what's up with this? I open wide, and he stuffs my panties between my lips. My eyes widen as my own taste fills my mouth. This is fucked up, and I love it.

"There's my good little fucktoy. Now your moans won't get us in trouble." The zipper on his pants sounds loud in the room. "Hands on the wall. Spread your legs."

As I turn around to face the wall, footsteps pass nearby, and my heart races. Anyone could hear us, but that only makes me wetter.

"Look at you," he chuckles darkly, pressing his cock against my entrance. "Getting off on this, aren't you? Such a desperate slut."

"Fuck yes, I am," I murmur around my panties, knowing he can't understand me. I try to push back, earning a sharp slap on my ass.

"Patience." His breathing is ragged. He thrusts hard, making me bite down on the panties to muffle my cries of pleasure.

More footsteps, voices discussing the morning sessions. He doesn't slow down, just fucks me harder.

"That's it," he grunts, one hand gripping my hip while the other slides around to rub my clit. "Take it like the fucktoy you are."

My eyes roll back as he hits that perfect spot. Jon's soooo going to love hearing about this later.

"Touch yourself," he orders, moving both hands to my hips. "Make yourself come on my cock like a good girl."

I reach down, finding my swollen clit. The angle's awkward, but fuck, I'm so close.

"After you come," he pants in my ear, "I want you on your knees. You're going to suck me off with that sexy mouth."

That does it. My orgasm rips through me, and I barely keep quiet with the panties gagging me. He shivers before pulling out and spinning me around. I drop to my knees, and he replaces the panties with his cock. "Suck it, slut."

Holy fuck. I moan, tasting myself mixed with his cum. His fingers wrap around my head, controlling my pace.

"Such a dirty little cocksucker," he growls. "You love this, don't you? Being used in a supply closet while everyone's at lunch?"

I hum my agreement, taking him deeper. His hips start to jerk, and I know he's close.

"Swallow it all." It's a command. I feel him pulse on my tongue, flooding my mouth with his cum. Like the good girl I am, I don't spill a drop.

Once he's done unloading, he helps me up and adjusts my shirt. There's a new softness in his eyes, but his voice stays firm. "Clean yourself up. Next session starts in ten. I have sandwiches for us to eat."

In the restroom I look at my balled-up panties with dismay. Fuck, what is worse? Sitting with no panties, or these? I clean up the best I can and put on my panties. The damp fabric makes me feel like a complete slut. It's filthy—and glorious.

I check my phone before I leave. There are two texts from Jon.

Jon:

> Having fun kitten?

Jon:

> Can't wait to hear ALL about it tonight

Oh babe, do I have stories to tell you.

CHAPTER 4

The afternoon speaker drones on, but I'm lost in a haze of desire. My body's still buzzing from our supply closet rendezvous, and Mr. Daniels' hand on my thigh isn't helping.

"Take notes," he murmurs. "This is important."

Important? I try to ignore the throb between my legs, but it's no use.

"After this, tell me three key points about the presentation." Mr. Daniels whispers, squeezing my thigh.

Shit, that voice makes my stomach flip. "Or what, sir?"

His smile is wicked. "Or I'll punish you in that empty meeting room down the hall."

My pussy clenches. Yeah, he's not deterring me. Now I might tank his quiz on purpose.

The presenter clicks onto another slide, but Mr. Daniels' hand inches higher, making me squirm.

"Desperate little slut," he breathes. "Still wet from lunch, aren't you?"

I cross and uncross my legs, seeking friction. "Please, sir…"

"Please what?" His fingers tease my sensitive skin. "Please bend you over the table? Please make you scream where anyone could hear?"

My clit throbs with each scenario. Jesus, he really is good at this—or else I'm just that turned on. Either way, today is going so much better than I imagined.

"Five minutes left," Mr. Daniels says softly. "Better pay attention if you want to pass."

I try to focus, but his hand creeps higher, his touch bolder. By the time the lights come up, I'm breathless.

"Well?" He turns to me, all business except for the heat in his eyes. "Three key points. Go."

"Um..." I scramble for answers, but my brain is mush.

His smile grows as I stumble. "Not good enough." He stands, straightening his jacket. "Come with me. Time for your punishment."

Thank god I'm such a terrible student.

Mr. Daniels leads me down the hall to an empty conference room like he promised. My pulse quickens as he shuts the door behind us, the click of the lock echoing in the silence.

"Bend over the table," he commands, and I practically stumble in my haste to get to the nearest table. I do as I'm told, leaning forward and placing my palms flat on the wooden surface. My skirt rides up, exposing my thigh-high stockings and the lace trim of my panties. When I look over my shoulder at him, the heat in his eyes intensifies, and my stomach flutters in response.

Mr. Daniels steps closer and runs a hand over my ass, squeezing gently before delivering a sharp smack. I gasp, the sting sending a jolt of pleasure through me. "You failed your test," he murmurs, landing another smack on the opposite cheek. "What do you have to say for yourself?"

"I'm sorry, sir," I breathe, my voice catching as he continues to spank me. Each strike sends a wave of heat through my body, my pussy throbbing with need. "I'll do better next time."

"Will you?" His hand slips between my legs to press against my clit through my panties. I squirm, desperate for more friction. "Or will you be a bad girl again?"

"I...I don't know, sir," I admit, my voice trembling. He chuckles, a low, throaty sound that makes my knees weak. His fingers delve deeper, pushing my panties aside and circling my clit before pulling away. I whimper as a shiver runs through me. Fuck, this is intense.

"On your knees," he orders, stepping back.

Does this mean he's not going to fuck me? I slide off the table, sinking to the floor. He unzips his slacks, freeing his cock. It's hard and thick, and I lick my lips, eager to taste him. He grips my hair, guiding me forward. "Show me how sorry you are."

I take him into my mouth, my tongue swirling around the head. He groans, his hips jerking slightly. I suck him deeper, my hands gripping his thighs for support. His skin is warm beneath my touch, the muscles taut with restraint. I can feel the tension building in him.

"Fuck," he groans, his voice strained. "Such a good little cocksucker."

Mmm, I'll suck on him all day if he calls me filthy names. I focus on pleasing him, my neediness building with each bob of my head. His fingers tighten around my head, controlling the rhythm. I can taste the saltiness of his precum, feel the throb of his cock against my tongue. He's close, I can tell.

He thrusts deeper into my mouth. I relax my throat, taking him in as far as I can. His breath hitches, and I can feel the pulsing of his cock as he nears the edge.

"I'm going to come," he groans, his voice ragged.

I double down on my efforts, my tongue working furiously. With a final, deep thrust, he holds me in place, his cock pulsing as he fills my mouth with sticky cum. I swallow every drop, trying to make up for not knowing the answer to his quiz.

He pulls out slowly, his breath coming in heavy gasps. I look up at him and he runs a thumb over my wet bottom lip, a satisfied smile on his face.

"Good girl," he murmurs, helping me to my feet. He tucks himself back into his slacks, adjusting his clothes with calm efficiency.

I'm buzzing with unfulfilled desire, and he kisses me softly. "If you're lucky, I'll fuck you again after the next session."

Oooh, yes, please. "I'll make sure to pay attention this time, sir." Though now that I think of it, I did like that punishment. Maybe I won't pay attention after all.

"You better," he says, giving my ass a final squeeze. "Now, let's get back. We wouldn't want anyone to know how much you enjoy being on your knees for me."

As we walk down the hall, my lips feel puffy and I grow hot every time someone looks at me. Yeah, I'm a slut and I actually do wish everyone knew how much I enjoyed being on my knees.

CHAPTER 5

During our afternoon break, I'm on my feet, ready to follow Mr. Daniels anywhere. He leads us to the front desk where he checks in—and he already has a reservation. When I give him a questioning look, he flashes a wicked smile. "I want to take my time, and I'm going to make you scream."

Damn. My pussy throbs at his words.

The elevator ride is delicious torture, and all I want to do is throw myself against him and beg him to fuck me right there. When the elevator open, I practically sprint down the hall.

He unlocks the door, and we step inside. It's just a standard hotel room, but right now, it feels like a sanctuary.

"Undress," he orders, leaving no room for argument—not that I was planning to put up a fight. I'm about to rip off my clothes but pause. Wait, this is my chance to drive him crazy.

I step out of my heels, and he watches with hunger as I begin a slow, sensual striptease. I unbutton my blouse, one button at a time, allowing it to slip off my shoulders before tossing it to the floor. My skirt drops next, and I'm standing in front of him in just my bra, panties, and stockings.

His eyes are glued to me, taking in every movement. I reach behind my back and unhook my bra, letting it fall. His gaze makes my nipples harden. I slowly roll my stockings down, one leg at a time, using my foot propped up on the bed to slide them off sensually. I finally slip off my panties, kicking them aside.

His eyes roam over me, taking in every curve. "Beautiful," he murmurs, stepping closer. He traces the curve of my waist, the swell of my hips. "And all mine right now."

He takes his time exploring me with his hands, like he's unwrapping a gift he's waited forever to open. His touch sets my skin on fire, and I shiver in pleasure.

I can tell when he's ready to fuck me. The tension shifts, and he commands, "On the bed. On your back."

I lie down, heart pounding as he undresses. His suit and shirt hit the floor, revealing his broad chest and defined abs. Fuck, he's stunning.

He crawls onto the bed, covering my body with his. His mouth finds my neck, kissing and sucking while his hands explore. I gasp as he pinches my nipple, rolling it between his fingers.

"I wish we had time for me to play with you all day," he murmurs against my skin. God, I wish that too. If this is what he'd be doing to me, he'd turn me into a mindless puddle by the end of the day.

His mouth moves lower, capturing one nipple, then the other, sucking hard enough to make me arch. My hands grip his hair as he focuses on my breasts.

"Please, sir," I whimper, not sure what I'm begging for. More teasing? Less? Everything?

He chuckles, a low rumble vibrating through me. "Patience, greedy slut."

His mouth trails lower, kissing down my stomach. I tense as he reaches my hips, anticipation coiling tight.

"Open," he orders, nudging my thighs apart. I comply, spreading wide for him.

"Fucking perfect." His eyes are locked onto my pussy. He leans in, his breath hot against me.

The first lick is slow, deliberate. A tease. I buck my hips, chasing his mouth, but he pins me down with a stern look.

"Stay still," he commands. "Or I'll stop."

Fuck. I force myself to obey, gripping the sheets as he licks me again, slow and torturous.

His tongue finds my clit, circling it lazily. I whimper, the sound turning into a moan as he sucks it into his mouth. He releases it, blowing gently on my wet flesh.

"Oh god," I gasp, hips trying to lift. His hands hold me down, his mouth driving me insane.

He slides two fingers inside me, pumping them in and out while his tongue works my clit. The dual sensation is overwhelming, pleasure building fast and hard.

"Sir, please," I beg, head thrashing. "I need to come."

He hums against my clit, the vibration sending sparks through me. "Not yet," he murmurs. "You'll come when I say you can."

Fuck fuck fuck. I close my eyes and tense up, trying to hold back my orgasm. He adds a third finger, stretching me wide. His mouth returns to my clit, sucking and licking until I'm a writhing, whimpering mess.

"Now," he growls, fingers curling inside me. "Come for me, slut."

My orgasm hits like a tidal wave, pleasure crashing through me. I scream, body convulsing as he wrings every last bit of ecstasy from me. When the pleasure dies down to soft ripples, he crawls back up, his cock poised at my entrance. In one hard thrust, he's inside me, filling me completely.

"Fuck, you feel good," he grunts, hips moving in a steady rhythm. "Like you were made for my cock."

I wrap my legs around him, meeting each thrust with a moan. His body against mine, his cock inside me—it's perfection. I can't believe how lucky I am to have a husband who lets me fuck other guys like this. Jon really is the best husband in the world—especially because I'm going to tell him how good this felt, and it's just going to turn him on even more.

Mr. Daniels captures my mouth in a fierce kiss. I can taste myself on his tongue, and it only makes me hotter.

"Touch yourself," he orders, breaking the kiss. "Make yourself come again."

My hand finds my clit, rubbing in time with his thrusts. Pleasure builds quickly, my body already sensitized from the first orgasm.

"That's it," he pants, eyes locked on mine. "Show me how much you love my cock."

I cry out, my second orgasm hitting just as hard as the first. He follows right after, his cock pulsing inside me as he finds his own release.

We collapse together, bodies slick with sweat. His arms wrap around me, holding me close as we catch our breath.

We lie there for a few minutes, basking in the afterglow, but Mr. Daniels breaks the silence with a stern voice. "You never did answer my question from earlier."

I look up at him, confused. "What question, sir?"

"The three key points from the presentation. I'll give you another chance. Give me three things."

I still can't think of anything, and I don't even try.

He looks amused, but his voice is stern. "You failed again."

A shiver runs through me, remembering the earlier punishment. "Yes, sir."

"On your hands and knees," he commands, his voice leaving no room for argument. "It's time for more punishment."

I scramble to obey, positioning myself on the bed, my heart racing. He gets off the bed and walks around to stand behind me. His hand caresses my ass gently at first, then suddenly, a sharp smack lands on my right cheek. I gasp, more from surprise than pain.

"Count them," he orders, his voice stern.

"One," I manage to say, my voice breathless.

Another smack, this time on my left cheek. "Two," I count, my pussy clenching with each strike.

He alternates between cheeks, each smack sending waves of pleasure and pain through me. I count each one, my voice growing more desperate with every number. By the time I reach ten, my ass is throbbing and I'm dripping wet.

He pauses, his hand resting on my heated flesh. "You took that so well," he murmurs, his voice thick with desire. "Such a good little slut."

I whimper, pushing back against his hand, craving more. He chuckles, a low, dark sound that sends shivers down my spine.

"Stay just like that," he commands, his voice rough with need as he climbs onto the bed behind me. His cock presses against my entrance and I moan when I feel how hard he is again. How the fuck did he recover that fast? I'm one lucky girl.

He applies pressure to my shoulders, shoving them down to the bed so I spread open wider for him. "Do you think you deserve to be fucked, slut?"

"Please, sir," I beg, desperate. "I deserve it. I'll be good, I promise."

"We'll see about that."

In one smooth motion, he buries himself inside me, stretching me impossibly wide. I cry out from the pain mixed with pleasure. He starts to move, his pace relentless, forcing every inch of his huge cock into me. His hips slam into my abused ass, sending a constant stream of white-hot lightening through me.

He fucks me deep and hard, his grunts punctuating each thrust. His fingers dig into my hips, holding me steady as he uses my body for his pleasure. I can tell that he's having fun, that he enjoys being in control, and the thought pushes me over the edge. I moan loudly, pleasure radiating from my fingertips to my toes.

"Yes, just like that." He slams into me harder, faster. "You feel incredible. Your tight little hole, all dripping and needy."

Whoa, my head spins as his words turn filthier. I really do want to be his hole to use. I let myself imagine that he's going to keep me restrained all day and come into the room and fuck me whenever he wants before going back to the conference, leaving me a dripping mess. I wouldn't even care if I didn't come.

He changes the angle, and his cock rubs against the magical spot deep inside me. My arms shake from the intensity, but he keeps pounding me into the mattress, chasing his release. It's glorious, and I don't want him to stop.

His pace becomes erratic, his grunts turning into groans. "Fuck, I'm close," he grits out, his cock swelling even larger. "Where do you want it?" He reaches around and rubs my clit while he keeps fucking me.

"In-inside me," I gasp, knowing that him asking me means he might not give me what I want if he has a sadistic streak in him.

He growls, "Good, because that's exactly where I planned to come."

Oh, thank god. He slams into me even harder, and I scream when a sudden orgasm rips through me. He fucks me through the pleasure before he groans and pumps me full of cum. My entire body quivers from pleasure while I imagine his cum coating my insides until I'm overflowing.

When he's done unloading, we both collapse face first onto the bed. My head is wooly, and I'm drunk on pleasure. Yep, I don't think I can move from this spot. I'm going to become one with the bed.

When I giggle, he rolls on to his side, facing me. I can tell he's looking at me, and I open the eye that isn't smooshed into the comforter so I can see him.

He's smiling. "You okay?" His voice is soft and caring. He's back to the Mr. Daniels I know.

I turn my head so I don't mumble into the mattress. "So much more than okay. That was incredible. You're incredible. Thank you for that."

His laugh is joyous. "You're amazing. Thank you, Miranda. But I think that's the last one I had in me."

I'm not sure I have another in me either. I have to save something for Jon when I get home. Though right now, maybe I'll just starfish and tell him to have at it. I keep that thought to myself and reply with a pout. "Probably for the best since I can't walk."

He laughs loudly as he gets off the bed and then pulls me into a sitting position. I pretend to be a limp noodle until it gets to the point where I have to support myself. "Up and at 'em, lazy bones. We need to get you home. I think we're going to skip the last session of the conference."

Oh, thank Jeebus. I give him a cheeky, "Yes, sir," as I climb off the bed.

I sink into the heated seat of his car as Mr. Daniels steers us out of the parking garage. My panties are shot, my nipples hard against my bra. I thought I was exhausted, but knowing I'll soon see Jon is waking my body up. It's still a couple of hours until he's off work, but I'll be more than ready for him when he gets home.

"Tired?" Mr. Daniels asks.

"Not really. Just processing, I guess." Processing how much he's changed in the last two years. God, I really hope Jon lets me keep fucking my bosses after this week. I need more of Mr. Daniels.

He chuckles. "It was quite a day."

Quite a day? That's an understatement. "I enjoyed it. A lot."

He gives me the side eye and a smirk before focusing back on the road. "Oh, I could tell. You're very...expressive."

I blush as a thrill runs through me. "Well, you weren't exactly quiet yourself, *sir*." I make sure to stress the word 'sir.'

"True enough. You have a way of bringing out the beast in me."

Mmm, and I do like his beast.

When we pull into the driveway of my house, he sighs. "Back to reality at the office tomorrow."

Wait, what? I don't want reality tomorrow. Plus, when do I get a day with Mr. Parks? I make a mental note to myself to make sure to ask Jon about anal with Mr. Parks since I keep forgetting and I know Mr. Parks will want my ass.

"But that doesn't mean this has to end," he continues. "We can find ways to make this work, if you want to and if Jon agrees."

If I want to? Fuck yes, I want to. But I appreciate he's considerate about my husband. "I'll talk things over with Jon and let you know."

Hrm, I wonder how many imaginary blowjob tokens I'll have to pony up to Jon if I want to keep fucking my bosses?

Mr. Daniels turns to me, his eyes soft in the dim light of the car. "Thank you, Miranda. For today, for trusting me, for being you."

I smile, my heart swelling with affection. "You're sweet, and thank you, too."

He leans in, his lips brushing mine in a soft, tender kiss.

"Goodnight, Miranda," he murmurs against my lips.

"Goodnight, sir."

Chapter 6

The front door clicks shut behind me, and I jump, startled to see Jon standing there. "Hey, you're home early!"

There's a fire in his eyes. "I took a half day. I couldn't concentrate."

Before I can even drop my bag, he's on me. He spins me around and pushes me against the wall. Fuck, yes.

"Tell me everything," he demands while his hands roam over my body, rough and possessive.

I gasp as he grinds his hard cock into my ass. "He shoved my panties in my mouth and fucked me in a supply closet."

Jon groans, his fingers digging into my flesh. "And?"

"And then in a hotel room. He made me come so hard I couldn't even stand."

"Fuck, kitten," he murmurs, his hands cupping my breasts and kneading them. "It's so hot when you talk like this."

When he pinches my nipples through my blouse, I moan, "Need you."

That's all the encouragement he needs. He hikes up my skirt and yanks my panties down to my ankles. I step out of them, kicking off my heels at the same time. I spread my legs. I need him inside me. Right now.

"Please, Jon," I whimper, my body aching for him.

"So fucking wet," he groans, running his fingers through my soaked folds. "Is this all for him or is some of this for me?"

"You. Always." It's a struggle to keep my words coherent through my moans.

He slams into me from behind, his thrusts hard and deep, his groans mingling with my cries of pleasure.

"Did he fuck you like this?" he growls, his pace increasing. "Did he pound you against the wall?"

"Yes, in the storage closet," I whimper. "Keep talking to me. Just like that."

"That's 'cause you're my slut who likes fucking other guys and coming home and getting it rough from me. Admit it."

Jesus Christ, why does this turn me on so much? "Yes, god, I do. I love it."

He keeps fucking me, and my head spins as he talks. "You love knowing that when I think about you fucking other guys, it drives me crazy, don't you?"

"God yes, I do!" This is the crazed Jon that I love coming home to.

"Do you think about that when you fuck them? Do you picture me listening to this story, turned on and ready to fuck your brains out as soon as you tell me what they did to you?" As he drives into me furiously, the pressure inside me coils tighter, his dirty talk bringing me closer to the edge.

"Yes!"

He bites the soft skin on my shoulder, and I almost come right there from the sting. A wave of lust makes me cry out, "Fuck me hard and show me who I belong to!"

Jon's response is immediate and intense. He pulls out, and I feel like a rag doll as he spins me around and lifts me until I wrap my legs around him. His face is a blend of dominance and ownership, and it sizzles my brain.

He crushes his lips against mine, his tongue claiming me as his own. He drills into me, and his grunts match my moans of pleasure. This man is perfect. We're both crazed, desperate for release. I hold onto his shoulders, letting him have total control.

My orgasm hits like a tornado, a swirling white-hot ecstasy that burns through me. I cry out as the pleasure skyrockets me to another plane. The feeling of him blowing his load inside me makes the bliss last even longer before it finally dies down to sparks. When I come down, I'm spent, unsure if I can even walk.

He kisses me deeply. The world seems to pause as we lose ourselves in the moment. This right here is one of the best parts. When he breaks off the kiss, he carries me into the living room. He lowers us both onto the couch, settling me comfortably in his lap.

Giggling, I nuzzle his neck. "Now that's what I call being well fucked. That was fantastic. Did you enjoy it?" I poke him in the ribs. I know he did, but I still like to hear him say it.

"I fucking loved it. Just like I love you." He's grinning, and a flush is riding high on his cheeks. His voice softens. "So, how was it really? I mean, beyond the fucking."

I rest my head on his shoulder. "It was...intense. And fun. I like how dominant Mr. Daniels is now."

He kisses the top of my head, his arms tightening around me. "Yeah, my slutty kitten would like that. I'm glad you had fun today."

My heart flutters. "Thank you for supporting me, for encouraging me. For loving me."

"Always, kitten. Always."

Later when we're making dinner together, my phone buzzes. It's a text from Mr. Jacobs.

Holy shit. My heart pounds as I read the message, my body already responding to the thought of fucking all my bosses together.

"What is it?" Jon asks, curiously.

I look up at him, my eyes wide with excitement. "They want to have an office party tomorrow. With all of them. At once."

Jon's expression darkens. "All of them? Together?"

I nod, his expression making me uncertain if this is a good thing. "Yes. But...we should talk about this first, right?"

He runs a hand through his hair, his expression unreadable. "Definitely. I love sharing you, kitten, but all of them at once...that's different. We need to discuss this before I can agree to something like that. I have rules."

My stomach flutters with a combination of disappointment and understanding. Will he say no?

God, I hope not.

The End

FREEUSE OFFICE PARTY

LACEY CROSS

CHAPTER 1

The car pulls up to the curb in front of the office, and my husband Jon kisses me goodbye. "Have lots of orgasms today, Kitten."

I give him my best cheeky grin. "One can hope."

But honestly, how can I not? It's the last day of freeuse at work before Cindy, the receptionist, comes back from vacation and we have to behave—or at least keep the sexy shenanigans behind closed doors. This week has been fabulous, but fairly intense. It might be good that she's coming back. I don't think much actual work was done this week.

I step out of the car, and smooth down my flared skirt before collecting my purse and lunch. Jon waves to me and I blow him a kiss before he takes off. He doesn't usually take me to work, but Mr. Jacobs offered me a party with all the lawyers today, and Jon is going to come back to watch. We're preplanning for once so we don't have two cars here, and he'll drive me home after the party...assuming the lawyers agree to Jon being there.

The office is eerily still like it's been every morning this week, the usual hum of activity replaced by an almost palpable tension. No one is around the reception area, but the hair on my arms raises as if someone is watching me. I expect one of the lawyers to pop out of their office and fuck me at any second.

I barely have time to set my purse down before my phone's intercom buzzes.

Mr. Jacobs' voice cuts through the silence. "Miranda, my office in five minutes."

I get an immediate jolt of adrenaline. "Yes, sir."

I straighten my blouse again, double-checking that the top two buttons are undone to show a hint of cleavage. Actually—I unbutton another one so that the lace of my pink bra is peeking out. Jon chose this outfit for me, and I know he'd approve.

Since I have five minutes to kill, I turn my computer on and put my lunch in the break room fridge. When I get to Mr. Jacobs' office, the door is open and he's sitting at his desk.

"Close the door." He's using his stern tone that makes me instantly wet.

I do as I'm told, and stand in front of his desk with my hands clasped, waiting for his next move.

"Are you ready for your last day as our freeuse office slut?" He leans back in his chair. His gaze travels over me, and I fight the urge to fidget. "If you please us today—if you're a good girl—we'll all fuck you after work in the conference room."

Hmm, does he REALLY want me to behave? I fight the urge to smile, and tilt my head to the side. "And if I'm not a good girl?"

Mr. Jacobs' lips twitch with amusement. "Then we send you home without an orgasm. Simple as that."

Wait, does this mean I won't come at all today until the party? This was not part of my mental plan. I bite my lip, considering. He's manipulating me, and we both know it. But I'm eager to play along. I want this—I want them. But we need to talk about Jon. Shit, he better be okay with Jon watching.

I undo another button on my blouse and trail my fingers along my collarbone, making sure Mr. Jacobs is watching. "All of that is agreeable, but Jon has a demand."

Mr. Jacobs raises an eyebrow and I know he's waiting for me to elaborate.

"Jon wants to watch." Nerves flutter in my stomach. This is a deal breaker. No Jon, no party. "He wants to be here when you all use me."

Mr. Jacobs' keeps his face neutral. "Watch, hmm?" he muses. "And what makes you think we'll agree to that?"

I shrug. "Because you want to fuck me more than you want to deny Jon the pleasure of watching. And let's be honest, you'll get off on him watching too."

At least I hope so. I don't actually know if Mr. Jacobs has an exhibitionism kink, but we did a conference room fuck-fest years ago with Jon watching over video, and everyone seemed to enjoy that–including Mr. Jacobs.

His lips twitch again, and I know I've hit the mark. He's amused by this—the negotiation, the power play. It's all part of the game.

"You're right, but I'm not going to make it easy for you. If Jon wants to watch, that's fine. But you have to earn it. Understood?"

My heart pounds from excitement. I'm not exactly sure what they'll ask of me, but I always revel in whatever kinky thing my bosses come up with. "Understood, sir."

He stands up and moves behind me. "Then let's start with a reminder of who's in charge."

His hands slide down my sides, fingers brushing lightly against my blouse. Even through the thin fabric, his touch sends tingles of electricity through me.

He turns me to face him. "Take off your blouse."

I comply, and unbutton it, letting it fall to the floor. His eyes dip to the pink lace of my bra, and my nipples instantly harden.

"Beautiful," he says, his gaze lingering appreciatively. With one fingertip, he traces the delicate lace, the featherlight contact raising goosebumps across my skin. A mischievous smile plays at the corner of his mouth.

"I think I'll keep this," he says, scooping up my blouse from where it fell. "You can spend the day just like this. Give everyone at the office something to truly appreciate."

"Yes, sir." I really hope no clients stop by the office today.

"Good. Now get to work. You have a lot to do before 5 p.m." I nod, turning to leave, but he stops me. "And Miranda? Don't disappoint us."

I glance back at him. "Wouldn't dream of it, sir."

There's an extra sway in my hips as I leave his office. Dang it, why didn't he spank me already? I probably should have been bratty to start the day off properly.

As soon as I'm at my desk, I pull out my phone and text Jon.

Miranda:

> Babe, the party is at 5. I have to be a good slut today, or no party.

His response is almost immediate.

Jon:

> Then I guess you better be the best office slut ever. I want to see you take on all the lawyers.

I don't even try to stop my laugh. This is going to be fun, but there's one thing I need to know. My fingers hover over the keypad, hesitating for a moment before I type out the question.

Miranda:

> What if one of them wants to fuck my ass?

I hit send and wait, drumming my fingers nervously on the desk. My pulse quickens as I think about having all my holes filled today. Anal's not an all-access pass kind of thing. After I crossed one of Jon's boundaries a few years ago, Jon and I have a deal. My ass is his territory, and he decides who gets the key.

My phone buzzes, and I glance down.

I'm willing to share my hole today because it's a special day.

A flush warms me. Jon's willingness to share this part of me today makes me feel even more cherished, in a messed-up way. My fingers fly over the keys.

I promise to make you proud. Love you so much.

My heart flutters with anticipation and affection. Today is going to be incredible.

CHAPTER 2

The clock on my computer says 8:30 a.m, and the day stretches out before me. I'm uncertain what to expect. Am I going to do real work today? I'd rather not, but I'm alone in my little corner and the office is quiet. If I'm going to work without my blouse on, the least they could do was be around to admire me.

My instant messenger on my computer pings.

Mr. King:

> Come to my office.

Oooh, thank god. I stand and adjust my skirt, acutely aware of how exposed I am without my blouse. What my bosses haven't found out yet is that I'm wearing matching pink panties, along with a black garter belt and stockings. A seam runs down the back of each leg, adding a touch of elegance. Jon wanted me to be a proper freeuse office toy today, and that included wearing fancy undergarments.

My black high heels sink into the carpet as I make my way to Mr. King's office. I should probably ditch the shoes at some point, but I want a couple of the lawyers to see me wearing them first.

Mr. King's door is slightly ajar, and he's seated at his desk. He doesn't speak until I close the door behind me.

"Lock it."

I want to give him a cheeky, 'yes, sir,' but I keep it in. He's the lawyer I've fucked the most at work recently, and I know his MO now. He has a sadistic streak and he likes to provoke my bratty side.

I lock the door and when I turn back to him, he's standing. I take a moment to admire his broad shoulders—there's just something about a guy in a tailored suit that revs my engine and now that I know what Mr. King can do to me? Oh yeah, me and my slutty pussy are willing to jump through a lot of hoops to get what he offers.

His gaze lingers on my breasts before scanning the rest of me. I can feel the slick, wet heat between my legs, and I ache to be touched.

"You look..." He pauses, his eyes narrowing as he takes me in. "Fuck-able."

I fight the urge to rub my thighs together in anticipation. "Thank you, sir."

Having a fabulous orgasm would start the day off nicely.

He smirks, and a longing pulls at my core. "Take off your skirt."

I deftly unzip my skirt, and let it pool at my feet. He's the first one who gets to see the garter belt.

"Turn around," he commands.

I pivot slowly, giving him the full view. When I'm facing him once more, I find his expression unreadable, a practiced blank slate from years of negotiations.

He moves behind me like a predator. His fingers graze my hip before cupping my ass. I moan softly at the contact, and my panties grow damp. Heck, at this rate, I'll have my orgasm before 9 a.m. and still have 3 more lawyers to go.

"You want to come, don't you?"

"Yes, sir."

He chuckles. "Too bad. You're not going to."

Dammit. I frown. "But—"

"No buts," he cuts me off, and the sharpness only makes me want him more. "You're here to please us, remember? And right now, it pleases me to deny you."

Fuuuck. He knows exactly what he's doing. It's infuriating and exhilarating. And by how wet my panties are now, I'm clearly getting off on this.

He gestures to a stack of folders on his desk. "File these for me."

I'm caught off guard by the sudden shift. "File them in the cabinet here?"

"Yes. You're going to work while I use you."

My thoughts whirl as I start sorting them alphabetically. I keep imagining him fucking me as soon as I reach for the bottom drawer, so I'm distracted enough that I keep fumbling the order.

He huffs impatiently and applies firm pressure to my shoulder, making me bend over his desk until my face is squished against the pile of folders. Yeah, okay, this wasn't exactly what I expected, but it'll do.

"You like knowing I can use you whenever and however I want, don't you?" I hear the clink of his belt buckle and the sound of him pulling down the zipper of his slacks.

"Yes, sir," I whisper, while a ping of excitement rushes straight to my pussy.

He nudges my panties to the side, the lace stretching as he exposes me. He positions the tip of his cock against my pussy, and I sigh and close my eyes as he thrusts into me slowly.

His thick cock stretches me wide, every ridge and vein massaging my slick pussy walls. I take him deeper and his hips press firmly against my ass. He doesn't rush—he fucks me slowly, each thrust measured, and I shake with the effort to hold back.

"You feel so fucking good." His voice is strained. "So tight around me."

He picks up the pace. Delight spirals from my pussy, but I know I can't come. Not yet. Not until he says so. It would just be momentary bliss, and then he'd find a new devious way to torture me.

He slams against me, and I yelp in shock and pleasure. The longer he fucks me, the more I stop caring about future punishment.

"Please, sir, I need—"

He cuts me off. "Oh, you need to come? That's unfortunate."

Damn him. My groan of frustration ends in a squeak as he smacks my ass. My eyes fly open. The sting creates a rush of ecstasy and I almost come all over his cock.

"Ooooh, god!" I cry out as he spanks me again, harder this time.

I grasp the side of the desk tighter and fight to hold back my orgasm. I don't want to risk punishment by coming.

"I'm going to use this tight pussy until I've had my fill. And then you're going to thank me. Do you understand?"

"Yes," I mewl out as he hammers into me. My cheek is still plastered against a manila file, and my vision swims from pleasure as I stare at the file cabinet across the room. If the plan was to make me a fucktoy first thing, Mr. King is doing a superb job of it. This is what I crave occasionally that my husband has a difficult time satisfying. I always know that Jon loves me. But Mr. King? Yeah, I'm being used. It's amazing.

"You're going to work like this all day," he growls as he pumps in and out of me. "Aching, desperate, and denied. And if you're a good girl, maybe—just maybe—you'll get to come at the end of the day."

I press my lips together, trying to hold back a whimper. He seizes my forearms, pulling them back and forcing me to rise up from the desk just enough that my nipples rub against the wood through my bra. The additional pleasure is almost my undoing as he fucks me harder.

His cock throbs inside me. He's close—I can tell by the way his breath hitches and his grip on my forearms tightens.

"Fuck, so good." He groans, a guttural sound, right before his cock pulses. He explodes, his hot cum filling me, coating my insides, and making me squirm.

He lets go of my arms to clasp my waist, holding me still while he unloads. I'm almost surprised when I don't come just from the warmth of his seed inside me. My pussy milks every last drop, as if draining his balls is my job.

"Good girl." His breath is ragged as he removes his cock. He slaps my ass and I don't even squeak. I'm too fuzzy-headed. "Now get back to work."

Oh god. I straighten up and look around the room. What am I even doing? I notice my skirt on the floor—oh yeah, I need that. I put it on and fasten it the best I can. I'll fix it later.

"Don't forget the folders," he grouses as he sits down at his desk.

My hands shake as I try to focus on gathering them into a pile. It's impossible. All I can think about is my throbbing clit and his cum dripping out of me.

"Mr. King," I say softly. "Please—"

He cuts me off. "Have you had breakfast?"

I blink in confusion, trying to recall the morning's events. Then I remember that Jon made me oatmeal and fruit before work, insisting I needed the energy for the day ahead.

"Yes," I reply, the memory of Jon's caring gesture warming me.

Mr. King nods and stands up. "Come with me," he says gently, holding on to my arm and leading me to the break room.

The change in his demeanor throws me off, but I follow without question. He grabs a bottle of water from the fridge and hands it to me. "You will drink all of this."

He escorts me back to my desk, his hand on the small of my back. He sits me down, his touch lingering for a moment before he pulls away.

"Drink up," he says, and then he turns and leaves.

I take a sip of the water, the cool liquid soothing my dry throat and perking me up a bit. It really did take me a bit to warm up to Mr. King when he joined the firm, but damn does that man know how to make me a submissive little slut. He ended up being the perfect addition to the firm.

The wetness between my legs and the way my damp panties cling to me are maddening. I'm going to be wrecked by the end of the day. And I can't wait.

CHAPTER 3

The morning crawls by, an endless tug-of-war between arousal and frustration. I cleaned up in the bathroom, but I swear that Mr. King's cum is still leaking out of me every time I shift in my chair. Yeah, it's probably just wishful thinking. After a trip to the copy machine, I kick off my heels—two of the lawyers saw me in them, and that's enough. My panties stick to my skin, the lace rubbing against my swollen pussy with each movement. I'm a needy slut, and it's barely past 11 a.m.

My instant messenger pings, providing a blessed distraction.

Mr. Daniels:

Come to the break room right now.

I try not to skip down the hall in excitement. Mr. Daniels is already there, leaning against the counter, arms crossed over his broad chest. He's not wearing a suit jacket, and I'm reminded again of how attractive he is. His rich, warm brown skin seems to glow under the break room lights, and he flashes me that amazing smile of his. His eyes, oh those eyes—crinkly at the corners and so full of lust—meet mine, and desire flutters in my stomach. After attending the conference with him yesterday, I'm looking at him in a new light. He's definitely grown more confident since he first joined the firm, which only makes him sexier.

"This is a delightful view," he says, his deep voice filling the room. His gaze travels over me, taking in my bra, my stockings, the way my nipples strain against the lace. "Come here."

I move closer, and he strokes my cheek with his fingers before trailing his hand down to my collarbone. His featherlight touch sends a shiver down my spine.

"I've been waiting for my turn with you all morning." His thumb tickles the skin on my breast just above my bra. "I hear you're being a good slut so far. So obedient."

"Thank you, sir." There's a fresh surge of wetness between my legs and I'm ready to worship his cock.

He chuckles, and turns me around, folding me over the break room table until I'm resting on my elbows. Oh, hello. He pulls my skirt up and presses up against my ass.

"I bet knowing that we can fuck you whenever we want today makes you wet."

"Yes," I whisper, and spread my legs in the hopes it entices him to take me right here.

His fingers slip beneath the lace of my panties, and he rubs my swollen clit. Jesus, if he doesn't fuck me soon, I'm going to go insane. He circles my clit slowly, his touch light and teasing. I clutch the side of the table and rock backwards.

When he inserts two fingers inside me and starts finger fucking me, I quiver as I try to hold back my orgasm. I'm peeping out in distress and the delight threatens to overwhelm me. "Oh, no, no. I'm going to come!"

He stills his hand and laughs. "No, you won't."

He removes his hand from my pussy and I almost groan. Fuck, this is worse.

"Come with me." He makes sure I can walk on my own, and I follow him to his office.

He shuts the door and sits at his desk. "Come over here and get on your knees. It's time for you to be a cockwarmer while I make a phone call."

Uh, fuck, that's hot. I sink to the floor in front of him, thankful I'm not wearing my heels any longer. He unzips his pants, freeing his cock, and I stare at his massive size. How did I get so lucky to work with four lawyers who all have impressive packages? Well, the real luck is that I have a husband willing to let me play with these gorgeous cocks. It's like winning the slut lottery.

"Open," he says firmly.

I part my lips, and he fits his cock into my mouth. I moan around him, the taste of his precum salty on my tongue. He presses on the back of my head, guiding my movements as I take him deeper. I relax, letting him fuck my mouth.

"That's it." He groans. "I always love using your mouth."

Always? Does he think about it outside of work? God, I hope he does. I moan in pleasure, the vibration making him twitch in my mouth. He twists my hair tighter, and suddenly, he holds my head still. His cock is still in my mouth but he's not thrusting.

He picks up his desk phone, dialing a number as I kneel there. I hear the ringing, and then a faint voice on the other end greeting him.

"Yes, this is Mr. Daniels," he says, sounding professional and calm, as if he isn't sitting there with his cock in my mouth. "I need to reschedule our meeting to next week."

My mind spins. I concentrate on not drooling on the cock occupying my mouth. This is humiliating, yet oddly exhilarating.

"No, Wednesday won't work." He shifts slightly, and I take the opportunity to change my position, trying to find a more comfortable angle. "I have a meeting scheduled with a client that day."

I curl my tongue around his shaft, and he grips my hair tight enough to make my scalp tingle. "Hold on a sec."

He presses mute on the receiver and looks at me. "Behave. You're just warming my cock. Don't even use your tongue."

Shit. I mumble, "Yes, sir," around his cock and then he unmutes the phone.

"I checked my calendar. Thursday works," he continues. "So, how have you been?" He now has a casual, friendly demeanor. "It's been a while since we caught up."

Oh god, what the fuck? I try to swallow, but some of my saliva runs down his cock. This is filthy, and I love it. I want to suck on him and clean him up, and just kneeling here while he chats as if he has no care in the world is the perfect blend of hot and annoying.

"That's great to hear," he says, laughing softly at something the other person says. "Yeah, we should definitely have lunch sometime soon." He ends the call and smirks down at me. "Okay, where were we?"

I hold still, waiting for him to give me instructions that I can move. He pushes my head down and I take that as a sign to start sucking again. I hollow my cheeks and get to work, but he takes over almost immediately and holds my head in one place as he flexes his hips to fuck my mouth. He groans at the moment his hot, salty release strikes the back of my throat. I struggle to swallow it all.

When he pulls me off his cock, I'm panting. He tucks himself back into his slacks. A mixture of cum and saliva spills down my chin. Quickly, I wipe it away with my fingers, then suck them clean, savoring every last bit.

He sighs, and I can tell he's pleased. My thoughts are jumbled. Jon is going to love hearing this part of the story.

He stirs and cups my face gently. "I think you've earned a reward."

I almost coo. Mmm, I like rewards. He lifts me to my feet and then boosts me up onto his desk. Oooh, is he going to fuck me? Can he even get it up again this quickly?

He forces me to lie back, but instead of fucking me, he sits down on his chair and drapes my legs over his shoulders. I gasp as he pulls my panties to the side.

His breath is hot against my pussy. "You're so fucking wet. I can see how much you need this."

"God, yes," I whimper.

He doesn't tease me and just dives in. I moan as he licks the length of my pussy and laps my clit. He devours me like I'm a five-star meal. My orgasm builds quickly, and I don't think I'll be able to stop it.

"Come for me." His voice is muffled against my pussy, but I'm still able to hear him. "Come all over my face."

As soon as he gives me permission, my orgasm hits. I'm drowning in a sea of bliss as he licks and sucks me through it. He's relentless and I'm almost too sensitive by the time he stops.

He stands up and wipes his mouth with the back of his hand. "You did so well, Miranda."

"Thank you, sir." I smile weakly, my body still buzzing with the aftermath of my orgasm.

He helps me sit up, and once he sees I'm steady, he says, "Now, clean yourself up. You've got more work to do today."

I hop off the desk and give him a little grin. "Yes sir, right away sir."

I sashay my way to the restroom. Thank god one of them let me come. I can think clearly after the orgasm, and my pussy tingles at the thought of what the next lawyer might do to me.

There's only five more hours until the party.

CHAPTER 4

I plop down into my office chair, my body humming like I've stuck my finger in an electrical socket. My bra feels too small, thanks to my tender breasts. Only one orgasm so far, and it's already past lunch. My bosses are playing hot potato with my libido, and I'm fairly certain all of them—except Mr. Daniels—are conspiring to keep me needy all damn day.

I peek at my phone, debating whether to shoot Jon a text. He's probably up to his elbows in work, but I know he'll want a status update. I unlock the screen and start tapping away.

Miranda:

> Babe, I've only come once. I'm dying over here.

I can almost hear his teasing tone when he replies.

Jon:

> Aww, poor kitten. Being a good office slut?

Miranda:

> The best. Oh, and they seem to be taking turns. Mr. Parks still hasn't fucked me.

Jon:

> Maybe he's got something special planned.

Hopefully it's his cock or fingers in my ass. As soon as Jon said he'd share my ass, I turned into my sluttiest self—well, let's be honest, I was mostly already there. But now all I can think about is having Mr. Parks' cock in my ass so I can drip cum from every hole.

Miranda:

> I don't need anything special, I just need more orgasms.

I pout, wishing he was here to appreciate my pain.

Jon:

> I love it when you get all cranky.

Miranda:

> You're the best. Now stop distracting me. I'm trying to work!

Jon:

> You do that, and don't spend too much time imagining me sitting here stroking while thinking about watching you get fucked by your bosses.

A thrill zips through me. He always knows how to rev my engine, even from afar. I doubt he's actually stroking at work...right?

I text him some heart emojis and stash my phone in my purse. Dang, I wish Jon were here right now and watching all of this, but we'll have fun for days while I tell him everything that happened. First, I have to survive the rest of the day.

Right on cue, my instant messenger dings. It's Mr. Parks.

Mr. Parks:

> *Come to my office.*

Hell yeah. A delicious ache between my legs roars to life as I head for his office. His door is closed, and I knock.

"Come in."

Mr. Parks is at his desk, and his glasses perched on his nose give him a sexy, geeky look. My pussy clenches like she thinks she's going to get spanked, and I almost giggle from excitement. Okay, so yeah, I've been really looking forward to spending time with Mr. Parks again. He's the only lawyer who hasn't fucked my pussy yet this week.

"Lock the door. We don't want anyone walking in on this."

Uh, yeah...probably not. But is one of the other lawyers going to really walk in? I do as I'm told, and then stand there at the door, fidgeting. I'm so desperate right now, I could just lie down on his desk and beg him to do me. I'm not sure I have coyness in me right now.

"Come here," he finally says.

I step closer, my legs wobbling slightly. He leans back in his chair, eyes roving over me and I'm tempted to turn around so he can admire me from behind.

"Are you ready for me to fuck your ass today?" His tone is almost conversational, which makes this all dirtier.

Happy butterflies swirl in my stomach, and I keep my answer simple. "Yes."

"Good." He smiles, and I expect him to tell me to bend over.

He doesn't.

"But first there's a quiz."

Uh, what? "Quiz?"

"If you answer correctly, you can come when I fuck your ass. Answer wrong..." He leaves the rest unsaid.

My brain's scrambled from the day's festivities. But heck, maybe they'll be easy questions. "Okay. Ready when you are."

He motions me over to him. "One more thing. You'll be giving me a blowjob during the quiz. Now get on your knees."

Well, there goes my chance of an orgasm. No way am I going to be able to think with his cock in my mouth. I kneel between his legs and he pulls his cock out.

I'm a thirsty slut and he doesn't even have to tell me to open my mouth. I drop down onto his shaft, relishing the musky taste of his hard length. I really am in office slut mode, and if one of them told me to crawl naked to the break room to suck his cock, I'd do it.

I close my eyes and spend a moment familiarizing myself with his cock again, and savoring how it throbs in my mouth. He sucks in a breath when I flick the tip of my tongue along the veins, and then tugs on my hair to make me release him.

"What's the capital of France?"

Oh, this is easy. "Paris."

"Correct." He fucks my mouth again for a few minutes before pulling out. "Chemical symbol for gold?"

I try to think. "Um... Au?"

He thrusts back into my mouth, holding me there as he uses me. When he pulls out, I'm wooly-headed and gasping for air.

"Final question. What's 2,417 times 24?"

I hesitate, my thoughts sluggish like I'm wading through mud. Math? Seriously? The numbers jumble in my head. "I... I don't know."

"Two out of three isn't good enough. You don't get to come." He stands up, his chair rolling back with a soft squeak. "Bend over the desk."

I stumble to my feet and do as he requests, turning my head and resting my cheek against the smooth wooden surface. Knowing in advance I won't come pings the part of me that loves being a fucktoy. Using my ass for his pleasure only is the right kind of wrong.

He runs a hand over the fabric of my panties and pulls them down just far enough to expose my ass. He doesn't bother unhooking my garters.

"Such a pity you won't come. I wanted to make you scream while I fucked your ass. But rules are rules."

I imagine how much ecstasy it would take to make me scream and my nipples harden. I mean, I might come...Fuck it, I'm going to come if I can.

I hear the click of a cap opening, and then feel the cool lube. He takes his time, circling my entrance with a slick finger, making sure I'm prepared. This reminds me of years ago, that first day he brought me into his office and found out I'd never had anal sex. He just teased me with his finger, and made me eager to try it.

One of his fingers stretches me out. I moan as he adds more lube and a second finger. He pumps in and out while I adjust to having something in my ass. His cock is against my thigh, and he smears pre-cum along my skin.

"Maybe I should make you beg for it in the ass."

It sounds like he's talking to himself, so I stay quiet while pushing back against his fingers. The pressure is always a little uncomfortable at first, but it quickly turns to delight. God, I want another orgasm. He needs to just stick his cock in right now.

When he moves his free hand down to rub my clit, I quiver from pleasure and finally crack. "Please, Mr. Parks, I need your cock in my ass." I'm not above begging when I want something.

He chuckles. "That's more like it. I love it when you're a slut for an ass fucking." He removes his fingers, and a moment later the blunt head of his cock is pressing against my back entrance. He enters slowly, stretching me open around his thick shaft. The burn of the initial penetration gives way to pleasure as he eases inside.

"That's a sexy sight."

I look back at him, and his eyes are fixated on his cock sinking into my ass. I get naughty pleasure from imagining how dirty that looks from his view.

He grunts once he's fully seated and pauses, letting me acclimate. I flex my ass muscles for funzies, and we both moan as he pulls all the way out. He thrusts back in quickly and I squeal from the delight. Shit, fuck, he needs to keep doing that.

"So tight, so perfect," he grunts as he fucks me steadily.

I can only focus on the increasing ecstasy, and I don't know how long he drills into me. Everything is amazing. I jiggle my ass, trying to get as much pleasure as I can. I have to come before he does.

He picks up speed. "That's it, take my cock like the good little anal slut you are."

His words are punctuated by the slap of skin against skin as he pounds into me. His cock drags along my inner walls, and I'm so close to coming. My clit throbs, begging for attention,

"Yes, I'm an anal slut. Use my ass however you want." I'm babbling, too turned on to care about how desperate I sound.

He withdraws again until just the tip remains inside me before slamming back in. The force of his thrusts rocks the desk, and I have to brace myself against the surface to keep from being shoved forward.

"Please, Mr. Parks, I need to come. I'm so close." I'm practically sobbing now, and trembling with the effort of holding back my orgasm.

"No coming." He reaches around to rub my clit, and I nearly scream in rapture. He circles the nub mercilessly as he continues to fuck my ass.

"Please, I can't hold back. I'm going to come." My pussy spasms around nothing, and I'm going to explode any second.

"Too late," he groans as his cock throbs. Oh god, noooo. His warm seed coats my insides, and I'm twitching from the stolen orgasm.

He pulls out and sits in his chair. "Fuck, that was good."

I can only whimper in response as his cum drips out of my well-fucked hole. At least I got that, even if I didn't come.

He pulls a container of wet wipes from his desk and I sigh in relief when he cleans me up. After he uses one on himself, he puts his cock back into his slacks and then helps me to my feet. I stagger a bit, and I hold onto his waist while he pulls my panties up.

"Now thank me for fucking your ass and not letting you come."

His words immediately make me more submissive and I give him what he wants. "Thank you, Mr. Parks, for fucking my ass. And thank you for not letting me orgasm."

His eyes crinkle with satisfaction. "Anytime, Miranda. Now get back to work before one of the other partners comes looking for you."

I nod, and as I head to the door, he calls out. "And drink more water and eat a snack. Keep your strength up for later."

"I will."

His cum leaks out of my ass the entire walk back to my desk. There's only one cock I haven't had inside me yet today. Is Mr. Jacobs going to fuck me before the party?

CHAPTER 5

At about 3 p.m. Mr. Jacobs intercoms me and tells me to come to his office. I haven't done much work all day. Between the lawyers using me, I sat at my desk and blanked out while imagining being spit roasted by them.

When I get to his office, one glance from Mr. Jacobs has my heart racing.

"Shut the door," he orders.

My breath catches as I close it. If he didn't plan on using me, he'd leave it open, right? Cause really, closing the door is just for show—it's another way for him to control me.

He's sitting behind his desk, and his eyes devour me. I squirm under his stare and heat blossoms in my stomach.

"I heard you were quite the little slut today."

I'm not sure how to answer. I was a slut, and it was wonderful. But I'm not sure if that's going to get me what I want, so I try to deny it. "N-no, sir. I was a good girl."

Heh, a good girl at being a slut.

"Strip."

Mmm, oh yeah, I'm getting fucked, but just as added insurance, I take my time removing my skirt, since he still has my blouse. I lift my foot onto the chair, and toy with the clasps of my garter belt before I unhook one of my stockings. Mr. Jacobs stares at my legs. I know what he wants—and I'm more than willing to give it to him.

Slowly, I roll down the silk stocking, and the smooth fabric glides over my skin inch by inch as I reveal more of my bare leg. His gaze tracks the movement, and I get a zing of pleasure knowing I have his full attention. I finally slip the stocking off my foot, letting it dangle from my fingers for a moment before dropping it to the floor.

I switch legs, repeating the process with the other stocking. The room is silent except for the soft rustle of fabric and my own heartbeat pounding in my ears. I can sense the heat of his stare, the anticipation in the air.

Next, I remove the garter belt and it joins the stockings on the floor. Reaching behind my back, I unhook my bra and let the straps slip down my arms. I hold the cups in place for a moment, prolonging the reveal, before letting the bra fall away completely.

My breasts are full, yet perky, and I pull at the nipples while he watches with lust. Oh yeah, he wants me as much as I want him. I saved my panties for last because I know how to get him riled up. I turn around, facing away from him and hook my thumbs into the waistband. I slowly pull my panties down, leaning forward to give him a clear view of my ass as the fabric glides down my legs. Stepping out of them, I kick them aside with a playful flick of my foot. For the finale, I shimmy my hips before straightening up and facing him.

The desire in his eyes matches my raw need. He stands up and moves behind me. "Bend over. It's time for your spanking."

Fuck yeah. I position myself at his desk, resting on my forearms so I can look over my shoulder at him. I wiggle my ass to tempt him. My breasts are heavy, my nipples tight, and everytime they skim across the cool surface of the desk, it sends sparks of pleasure straight to my throbbing clit.

"Spread your legs," he orders, and I widen my stance.

His hand strikes my flesh, sharp and sudden. I gasp, the sting spreading like wildfire. He waits a beat, then strikes again. Each smack is a jolt of pain that melts into pleasure while my nerves sing.

As he continues to spank me, the tension increases in my core while my breath comes in short gasps. Each impact of his hand resonates through me.

"You're such a good little slut."

The praise makes me tingle and amplifies the delight. He changes his rhythm, alternating between sharp smacks and gentle caresses. The contrast drives me insane until I'm dizzy with need.

Each smack brings me closer to the abyss. A final, firm spank sends me spiraling. I cry with my climax, and pleasure radiates to my fingertips and toes.

His hand stills, resting gently on my heated flesh. "Good girl."

I am a good girl. I'm in a contented haze from the afterglow, and I barely register the rustling fabric as he takes his cock out. He positions himself behind me, and enters me with a single, powerful thrust. I moan as I almost come again. He was my first introduction to being a hotwife many years ago, and the fact that I'm allowed to fuck him again years later is surreal. I've changed since that first time—we all have—but somehow he still knows what I need.

He drives into me and each thrust creates waves of rapture. He reaches underneath me with both hands to play with my breasts, and he lifts me up slightly so he can roll my nipples with his fingers while fucking me.

"Ohhhh god," I moan as I try to fight against coming.

The tension coils again, but just as I'm about to come, he slows his movements. The change in pace leaves me teetering, the orgasm just out of reach. I moan in frustration as he continues to fuck me slowly.

"You don't get to come again," he growls.

Fuckity, fuck, fuck, fuck. He speeds up, and groans when he finally unloads. Pleasure zips through me, but it stops just shy of sending me over the edge. He fucks his cum back into me, and when he's done, it drips down my inner thigh. Oh yeah, I'm a mess, and going to get even dirtier soon.

I'm an odd mix of happy and frustrated when he says, "Work the rest of the day naked. No point in putting clothes back on."

Uh...other than I need my filthy panties to soak up his cum, but I don't argue. I'm not going to do anything that jeopardizes this party—especially knowing he just came and he might be willing to forgo the festivities if I get cranky.

I give him my best cutesy, "Yes, sir," and saunter out of his office, putting an extra sway in my hips for his benefit.

Is it time for this party yet?

CHAPTER 6

The clock hits 5 p.m. and my stomach flutters with excitement. Mr. Jacobs told me to bring Jon back to the conference room once he arrives.

I'm standing up and leaning against my desk when Jon enters the office and finds me. I'm going to keep my personal shame of sitting on a bunch of paper towels for the last hour to myself. They're in the garbage can, so he won't see them.

Jon's eyes widen a fraction when he sees that I'm naked. "Fuck, kitten. You're a goddamn vision."

His approval boosts my confidence. I'm a sexual goddess. "You like?" I turn slowly, giving him the full view.

"More than like." He steps closer, pulling me into a hug. "I'm obsessed. And I'm going to enjoy watching them fuck you before I take you home and remind you that you're mine."

Mmm, I love it when he gets all growly and possessive. He's going to be really worked up when this is over.

I blush with excitement. "They're waiting for us."

"Then let's go."

I lead him to the conference room, even though he knows exactly where it is. The door's open and as we walk into the room, I notice the lights are dimmed. The large table has been moved aside to create an open space. Mr.

Jacobs, Mr. King, Mr. Daniels, and Mr. Parks are perched casually against the table perimeter and all eyes are fixed on me.

"On your knees, Miranda," Mr. Jacobs commands, stepping forward.

Oh damn, they're not wasting any time. Jon moves over to a chair that is conveniently placed against the wall to give him a great view of the entire room.

I kneel down gracefully—I've had years of practice by now. Yeah, I'm on my knees often since I love sucking cocks. I lick my lips and study the bulge in Mr. Jacobs' slacks.

"Here's how this is going to go. You're going to suck on each of us, and then we're going to use you however we want because you're still our freeuse slut. You might orgasm, you might not, but you don't have to ask permission."

Okay, yeah, this sounds good. They use me and I can orgasm. I nod quickly and his eyes twinkle.

"And remember you can always use your safeword if this gets too rough."

I appreciate the reminder, but I already know from past experiences that I'm going to love everything they do to me. "Yes, sir."

Mr. King comes over, and takes his cock out of his pants. I guess Mr. Jacobs isn't going to go first like I assumed.

"Open."

My jaw drops down, and I welcome Mr. King's velvety-smooth cock into my mouth. I can see Jon to the side and he's leaning forward with his elbows resting on his knees, a rapt audience.

Being the center of attention, being used and desired, awakens every nerve in my body. I moan around Mr. King's cock as he fucks my throat. The tang of his precum is pleasant and I lick and suck on him, trying to see if I can make him come.

He pulls out before he does, and I pout. Yeah, my new goal is to make one of them blow their load in my throat when they didn't mean to.

Mr. Daniels is next, and I'm hungry for him. The men are only pulling their cocks out and not fully stripping, which somehow seems filthier. He barely has his out before I throw myself onto it with gusto. He grips my head firmly, forcing me to slow down as he guides me.

Again, the feeling of being used gives me a rush of delight. I know there is affection between us all—even me and Mr. King—but it's different from when Jon uses my mouth. Even though we've talked about boundaries, there's a tiny bit of uncertainty when I allow the lawyers to use me, which makes it even hotter. But having Jon here allows me to relax and really let go.

Mr. Daniels releases his grip to pull his cock out, and I'm left panting, my lips swollen and slick. Jon's gaze is on me. He's enjoying this and knowing that this is turning him on gives me an illicit thrill.

Mr. Parks steps up, his cock already hard and ready. He traces my lips with the head of his cock, teasing me. I dart my tongue out, trying to capture him, but he pulls back. "Eager, aren't you?"

"Please," I moan.

He holds my chin, tilting my head back before feeding me his cock. He's gentler than the others, his movements more controlled, but no less dominating.

My nipples tighten and my pussy spasms. I want more—need more. I ball my hands into fists and hold them against my thighs. Mr. Parks strokes my cheek softly before pulling his cock out without coming.

Mr. Jacobs is last. He puts his hands on my head, and guides me as he thrusts slowly into my throat. I gag slightly, but I'm able to take him. He fucks my mouth steadily, using me for his pleasure.

Jon's gaze is like a physical touch, searing my skin. It spurs me on, makes me want to take more, be more. I'm needy and aching to be fucked.

Mr. Jacobs pulls out, and a string of saliva sticks to his cock. I look up at the four of them, pleading. "Please fuck me."

They smirk and exchange looks. They know they have me right where they want me—aching, needy, theirs to use.

"I think the freeuse toy forgot that she doesn't get to decide how and when we use her."

It's Mr. King who speaks up and it takes all my willpower not to shoot daggers at him with my eyes.

"I'm sorry, sirs. Please, will you fuck me?" My words are soft and submissive, and I hope they're satisfied.

"That's a better attitude," Mr. King says. "On your hands and knees."

My heart thumps as I shift from kneeling to all fours. They circle me, and anticipation swirls in my stomach. I'm trembling by the time Mr. King kneels in front of me and Mr. Parks behind. Mr. Jacobs and Mr. Daniels lean against the conference table, watching.

Mr. King slides his dick back into my mouth while Mr. Park teases the entrance of my pussy with the head of his cock. I'm so desperate, I want to fuck myself on his cock, but I know better.

"Please," I whimper around Mr. King's shaft. I'm not sure which of them I'm talking to, but I don't care what they do as long as I orgasm.

Mr. Parks pushes inside me, and I'm so wet that he bottoms out easily. I moan as my body stretches to accommodate his cock.

Mr. Parks doesn't waste a second and he fucks me hard and fast. My pussy quakes as his balls slap against my clit.

He spanks my ass. "Don't move."

I'm so close, I'm not going to last much longer. I try to focus on sucking on Mr. King's cock, but it's impossible when Mr. Parks is pounding me so hard that it's shoving Mr. King's cock further down my throat.

"Look at our little office slut," Mr. Daniels says. "She's going to make you come, isn't she, Mr. Parks? It's amazing when her pussy flutters around me when I'm fucking her."

His filthy words make me moan. I love how degrading it is when they talk about me like I'm just a sex toy. I spent too many years wondering what was wrong with me for wanting this, and embracing this sluttiest side of myself is so fucking wonderful.

Mr. Parks' cock twitches. Oh god, yes, please fill me up. Every fiber of my being is focused on the impending ecstasy. My clit throbs and my nipples ache. I'm a live wire, the sparks threatening to ignite with each thrust.

"Come for me, Kitten." Jon's voice cuts through the fog of my lust.

That's all I need. I scream around Mr. King's cock as my orgasm crashes over me. Pleasure wracks my body, and I'm still coming when Mr. Park's hips stutter momentarily before he slams his cock into me one last time. His hot seed flooding me triggers a new wave of delight.

I'm lost in a sea of ecstasy when Mr. King explodes. I lose control and I can't swallow fast enough. Drool and cum leaks out of the sides of my mouth. I'm completely overwhelmed.

I'm still floating on a cloud of bliss when Mr. King pulls his cock out. The cool air of the conference room brushes against my heated flesh. I can't stop smiling. I'm a well-fucked slut, and it's not over yet.

Mr. Parks withdraws from my pussy, and his cum dripping out of me makes me shiver.

Mr. Jacobs speaks. "Clean him up."

Oh shit. I clamber to my knees again. Mr. Parks stands in front of me with his spent cock covered in our combined wetness. I lick from his balls up his shaft, tasting myself on him. He's still sensitive and I smile when his cock twitches.

Once I've given him a thorough tongue bath, Mr. Parks tucks his cock away and moves aside. Mr. Jacobs calls me over and then pushes me down on the table's surface. My nipples graze the wood as I rest on my elbows.

Mr. Jacobs slides his cock into my pussy. "Fuck, she feels so good."

He pounds into my pussy, and his cock drags against my inner walls. I moan loudly from the pleasure.

Mr. Daniels moves to stand next to my head, and he reaches out to stroke my hair. "You're such a good little office slut." He glances at the other partners. "I wonder how many times we can make her come."

That's it. Mr. Daniels is my favorite lawyer at the moment.

Mr. Jacobs grabs my arms and pulls them behind me. He holds them up and pivots, forcing me off the table so I'm facing Mr. Daniels. Mr. Jacobs picks up speed, and his hips slap against me. My pussy quivers, and I cry out and go limp as another orgasm skyrockets me to another plane of existence.

When I come back to earth, Mr. Daniels' cock is at my mouth, and I gurgle happily around his shaft. Mr. Jacobs grinds against me as he pumps my pussy full of his cum. I'm trembling, and I start wondering how much of this I can take. Can there be too much pleasure?

Mr. Jacobs pulls out, and Mr. Daniels withdraws from my mouth without coming. Mr. King takes over. I'm a rag doll as he moves me over to the table again, sitting me on top of it. Mr. King glides his hand up my thigh, his thumb circling my clit in delicate strokes. I melt against his hand and wrap my legs around his waist, hoping to draw him into me. He laughs and removes his hand and unhooks my legs.

"No you don't. I decide how I'm fucking you."

I rest back on the table while he folds my legs towards my chest. My ass is at the edge and he burrows into my wetness.

"Fuck, so good." He starts pounding me, his eyes fixated on where we're joined.

I'm still tender from my last two orgasms and it doesn't take long before I'm wound tight, my breath coming in shallow gasps.

"Oh god, I'm going to come," I cry out right before my orgasm washes over me. I'm lost in ecstasy, my fingers clawing at the table, seeking something, anything, to ground me. I can't hold on, can't fight against the wave of pleasure that consumes me.

Mr. King fucks me frantically, his cock swelling inside me and then exploding. He twitches as he pumps his cum into my well-used pussy.

When Mr. King pulls out, Mr. Jacobs moves between my legs. "One more," he says, sliding into me. "You can give us one more orgasm."

I can only moan in response. He's not wrong, and within minutes of him fucking me, I'm creaming all over his cock. I'm limp when Mr. Daniels picks me up and carries me over to a chair. He stands me up before sitting down himself.

"Ride me and fuck yourself on my cock."

I can do that. I face the room and lower myself onto his cock. Oh fuck. I'm not going to be able to walk straight tomorrow.

I'm so damn satisfied that it's hard to bounce on him, but I find a rhythm. Every nerve ending is pinged by his thick cock, and I'm not going to last long. He grasps my ass and lifts me up. Jon has a clear view of the chair and I play with my nipples while I fuck myself on Mr. Daniels' cock. Each tweak of my nipples sends a corresponding burst of pleasure from my clit, and my continual moans of "Oh god," are getting louder with every thrust.

"Come on, slut. You've got this." Mr. Daniel's voice is tight and he's clearly trying to hold back his own release.

He reaches down to play with my clit, and I shatter. My pussy quakes around him and I scream out. His cock pulses and he comes, adding to the collection of cum inside of me. I slump back against him, my head resting on his chest as I try to catch my breath.

I've lost count of my orgasms. I'm sweaty, sticky, and cum-filled. And I've never felt better in my life.

Jon pipes up from his chair. "One more time, Kitten. And guys, stuff all her holes."

Ooooh, god. Jon is nasty, and I love it.

Mr. King lies on the floor and they maneuver me over him. His cock is out and I sink down onto him. Fuck, my pussy is sore, but it still feels wonderful. Mr. King's cock stretches me again as I ride him slowly, enjoying the pings of pleasure and knowing there's more to come.

Mr. Parks produces a bottle of lube from his pocket and I lean down to give Mr. King a kiss while Mr. Parks preps me for his cock. My tongue twines with Mr. King's while Mr. Park works the lube into my ass. Within moments, he presses his cock against the tight ring and slowly inserts it. I moan into Mr. King's mouth from the intense pleasure. It takes a bit, but once he's inside me, I'm so fucking full, I feel like I could burst.

This is what happiness feels like, and that connection with Jon is unwavering even with me having two cocks in me right now.

"You good, Kitten?" Jon's voice is raw with emotion.

"So good."

When Mr. Daniels kneels next to me with his cock out, I swallow him down. This is the ultimate fantasy. Three lawyers in all my holes. The guys all fuck me and the pleasure makes my head spin. I didn't think I had another orgasm in me, but this is taking me to a place I've never been before. All my nerves sing in delight and it's heavenly.

"I think she needs all our cum at once," Mr. Daniels says, as he pulls out.

I don't know how they plan to do that, but at this point, I don't care what they do to me.

"Do you want to be covered in cum, slut?" Mr. Jacobs asks as he steps up next to me.

"Yes, please." I want it all. I want to be marked by them, to wear their cum on my skin. They have me so turned on that I might orgasm the moment they cover me in cum.

"Then beg for it. Tell us how much you want it." Mr. Jacobs commands.

I look up at him from under my eyelashes. "Please, I need your cum. Cover me in it." Begging the lawyers for their cum drops me into the darkest recess of my soul. A place where I'll do or say anything. "I'm a filthy office slut, and I'm here to be used. Please use me and paint me with your cum." I'm begging, the words pouring from me in a torrent of need.

Mr. Jacobs seems satisfied and says, "Open wide."

I obey, ready to take whatever he gives me. Mr. Jacobs eases into my throat, and as he thrusts into my mouth, the other lawyers focus on me. Their hands roam over my body, teasing and tweaking my nipples, stoking the fire that threatens to consume me.

Mr. Daniels stands next to me, holding his cock over my head while he strokes it. Mr. Jacobs fucks my mouth, and the rhythm of the thrusts in my ass are timed perfectly with Mr. King's cock in my pussy. I'm blissed out from the pleasure. Mr. Daniels' hand moves faster on his shaft and my skin tingles in anticipation of his hot cum on me. I'm so close, my orgasm is just within reach.

Mr. Jacobs' cock twitches as he nears his climax, his grip on my hair tightening. All the guys speed up their movements. Mr. Daniels' hot cum splashes on my face first. His release is the catalyst that triggers the others, and they're quick to follow. Mr. King and Mr. Parks groan and I feel my pussy and ass filled with cum as they explode deep inside me. It triggers my orgasm, and I cry out as my climax rips forcefully through my body. It's a soul-shaking orgasm that leaves me breathless and trembling.

Mr. Jacobs pulls out of my mouth at the last minute and aims for my chest. I shudder when his cum lands on my breasts, dripping down to my belly and thighs.

"Fuck," Mr. Daniels groans, his cock still spurting. His cum drips down my face and sends shockwaves of delight through me. I'm a filthy, cum-covered slut.

When Mr. Parks withdraws from my ass, he helps me climb off Mr. King. They leave me kneeling on the floor and they all step back, admiring their handiwork. I'm a canvas of desire, painted in their pleasure. It's glorious.

"Thank you." My voice is hoarse and I'm not sure if it's from all the cocks I had down my throat, or if it's from my moaning.

They chuckle, their gazes filled with satisfaction. "You're very welcome," Mr. Jacobs says. "We'll see you Monday, but unfortunately with Cindy back we'll have to be discreet if you want more fun."

Mmm, more fun. Jon and I will have to talk about that first. I giggle as the lawyers straighten their clothes. I'm tired and could lie down right here and sleep, but I force myself to stay on my knees.

The lawyers pause over by Jon, but I'm too addled to process what they're saying other than I hear them thank him for sharing me this week. Well, that's nice and respectful after such a filthy event.

Once they're gone, Jon kneels in front of me with a container of wet wipes that one of them must have given him. He cleans me up, and I giggle again as he wipes the cum off my face.

"You're a mess, Kitten," he laughs with me.

"Mmm hmm." I'm floating in my happy place, and indulging in the filthy sensation of their cum drying on me.

When Jon gets up and retrieves my clothes from a chair, I realize one of the lawyers must have put them there without me noticing. Jon dresses me like I'm a doll, all except my garter and stockings. It's sweet.

I'm a sleepy, happy little office slut, and I lean against Jon as we leave. "I love you, Jon."

He kisses the top of my head. "I love you too, Kitten."

Once we're in the car, Jon turns to me. "That was the hottest fucking thing I've ever seen in my life. Thank you."

"Mmm, I'm glad you enjoyed watching." I snuggle into the passenger seat. "I enjoyed the doing."

I close my eyes and drift.

CHAPTER 7

I blink and we're home. If someone had asked me back at the office if I was ready for Jon to fuck me, I would have said no, but the cool air as I step out of the car revives me, and just looking over at Jon's strained expression sends a bolt of desire straight to my core. I'm still humming from the aftermath of the office party, but there's a new energy inside me, one that's reserved only for him.

The moment we step into the house, Jon presses me against the wall and his mouth crashes onto mine. His kiss is demanding, and I melt into it, responding instantly. His tongue twirls with mine, and I can taste his urgency, his need to reclaim me.

"You're mine," he growls. "Mine to love. Mine to protect."

"Yes, yours," I whisper.

"I'm going to fuck you, Kitten. Hard. And you're going to take it because you belong to me."

"Yes, Sir. Please."

Oooh, hell yeah. Beast Jon came out to play. In my most honest moments, this is exactly why I love being a hotwife. I get railed by other men, and then Jon usually goes crazy and gives it to me hard.

He turns me around, pressing my breasts to the wall. His hands caress down my thighs and he hikes my skirt up. He grinds against my ass and I push back, trying to get him inside me.

He slaps my ass sharply, and I yelp from the pleasurable sting. "Who do you belong to?"

"You, Sir," I breathe out. "Only you."

"That's right," he growls while he moves my panties aside. He finds my clit and rubs it until I'm quivering from pleasure. My hands are flat on the wall and I use it as leverage to try and force his fingers inside me.

"Oh god, just fuck me. Please?"

"Oh, Kitten, I plan to," he laughs and pulls his hand out from between my legs. He quickly removes my clothes, dropping them in a pile on the floor. I step out of my heels as he continues. "But let's be clear on one thing…"

He doesn't complete his thought and he picks me up and carries me to the bedroom. He tosses me gently onto the bed and I watch as he strips.

Once he's naked, he crawls over me and nibbles on my neck. "I have two holes to reclaim."

Oh god, I'm about to have my ass stuffed full. "Yes. God, yes."

He sits back on his knees. "Spread your legs."

I eagerly part them and he nestles against me, his cock hard and thick, the tip already glistening with pre-cum. He teases me, rubbing the head of his cock against my clit before lining himself up with my entrance.

He pauses, holding back. He knows how to drive me wild, to make me ache for him, and I'm ready to explode by the time he finally slides inside me.

"Fuck," he groans, his cock stretching me open. He fills me perfectly, and having him inside me is a comfort.

He starts out slow, as if he's reacquainting himself with every inch of my body. I moan as he fucks me, my fingers digging into the sheets. I wrap my legs around him, urging him deeper.

Jon picks up the pace, and I cry out in pleasure from each thrust. He captures my lips in a searing kiss, and my tongue twirls with his. I'm lost in a sea of bliss as he trails kisses along my neck. I'm drowning in him—in us.

He reaches down to find my clit, his fingers working in time with his thrusts. "I want you to come on my cock, Kitten. Now."

It's all I need to fall over the edge. My orgasm crashes over me, my pussy clenching around his cock as waves of delight wash over me. I scream his name, my body quivering with the force of my climax. He continues to pound me through it, his own moans of pleasure mixing with mine. The rapture doesn't end, but just keeps climbing. I'm going to have another orgasm, and soon, and I'm not sure how that's even possible.

He pulls out, and before I can protest, he flips me over and tugs my hips up so I'm on my knees and elbows. His hands are on my ass, spreading me open. He has a bottle of lube. He obviously likes to be prepared. The gel is cold, and I jump as he coats my opening.

"Relax, Kitten," he murmurs as he pushes a finger into my ass. He moves it in and out of me before he adds a second. "You're taking my fingers like a good girl."

"Mmm, so good, Sir."

"I bet," he laughs as he adds a third finger, stretching my asshole to get me ready for him. "I think you're ready."

"Yessss." The word comes out in a long, drawn out hiss.

His lubed fingers leave my ass and the tip of his cock replaces them. "Breathe, Kitten."

I exhale and he pushes inside me. I'm so relaxed from being fucked all afternoon that his cock slides past the barrier easily. He doesn't stop until he's fully sheathed in my ass.

The pleasure is overwhelming. He tugs on my hair gently, and pulls my head up. I have to brace myself on the bed to stay steady. His other hand moves around to my front and he plays with my clit. I'm so sensitive that it hurts, but in the best possible way.

"Such a good girl," he says, his hips moving in small circles, his cock stretching my ass. "I think you can come like this."

I'm not sure I can, and I don't know if I could handle another orgasm. He's not giving me a choice, and I whimper as he thrusts and rubs my clit.

"Come again. Show me who you belong to."

His fingers are relentless on my clit, and I'm on the brink, the pleasure bordering on pain. I want to give him what he wants, but I'm not sure how much more I can take. I'm writhing, my breath ragged as the pressure increases.

"Please." I'm unsure what I'm even asking for, I'm so mentally fucked.

He slows down, but he doesn't stop. "You can do this, Kitten. I believe in you."

His fingers on my clit are short circuiting my brain. My body is on fire and I can't stop it. I don't want to stop it. I want to come apart, to surrender completely to him. I need to give him everything.

The pleasure crests and I scream his name as I come. Waves of ecstasy wash over me, each one more intense than the last. Jon's rhythm falters and he thrusts once, twice more and then stills inside me. He holds me in place as he comes, his cock pulsing in my ass as he fills me. The world fades away, leaving only the two of us.

I collapse onto the bed and he gently pulls his cock out and then lies next to me. He strokes my back gently. "I love you," he whispers. "You're always so good for me."

I'm floating in the haze, and I can't keep the smile off my face.

"You did such a good job today. You made me very happy. I'm so proud of you." He keeps telling me all the ways he loves me and I practically purr with contentment. He's always so sweet and loving after he reclaims me.

I'm drifting to sleep, his words wrapping around me like a warm blanket, his touch a gentle reassurance. He's the only man I love.

"You're mine, Kitten, no matter who I share you with."

"Mmm, yours," I murmur.

He kisses my shoulder. "Sleep a little but then you need to eat."

"Okay, love."

Everything is as it should be, and as my eyelids close, I know that Jon is my forever. Even if he decided to never share me with my bosses again, I'd still love him for all eternity. And I know he loves me the same way.

The End

ABOUT LACEY CROSS

Lacey Cross is a wife sharing erotica writer with over 100 short stories published since she started in 2021. Her stories emphasize the pleasure found from the wife living her best slut life and embracing the hotwife lifestyle. She explores themes of free use, submissive wives with dominant bulls, BDSM...and oh-so-many men.